GRAVE MISTAKE

GRAVE MISTAKE

AN IRIS REID MYSTERY

SUSAN CORY

Grave Mistake © 2023

Print Edition

Published by Susan Cory

The book is a work of fiction. Names, characters, places and incidents are either products of the author's imagination or are used fictitiously. Any resemblance to actual events or locales or persons, living or dead, is entirely coincidental.

All rights reserved. Except as permitted under the U.S. Copyright Act of 1976, no part of this publication may be reproduced, distributed or transmitted in any form or by any means or stored in a database or retrieval system or fed to AI, without the prior written permission of the publisher.

ISBN: 979-8-9871784-3-0

1

Iris Reid grabbed her keys and jammed her arm into the sleeve of her jacket, a piece of toast clamped between her teeth. She couldn't be late getting to her new office now that she had actual employees waiting for her. Her new commission to design a career-defining museum in Harvard Square finally broke through her reluctance to rent a larger space and hire staff.

Iris clipped a leash on Sheba, her eight-year-old Basset hound, and hoisted the unwieldy dog into the passenger seat of her new car. Sheba responded with a baleful look. No time this morning for the customary fifteen-minute walk to the office.

Reid Associates was located on Garden Street in a former furniture store, with large plate windows lining the sidewalk. Iris had been watching the real estate pages and snapped up the single-story brick building as soon as it came on the market. Six parking spaces in the unpaved back lot were included—pure gold in busy Cambridge.

It was only 9:05, but the office was already buzzing. Loretta

Jackson, her new receptionist/office manager, was seated at a narrow desk. She wore a headset with a blinking blue light, her fingers flying across her keyboard. She was thirty, a full fifteen years younger than Iris, but exuded the calm, efficient presence of a mother hen. A colorful mother hen with multiple piercings, turquoise-tipped cornrows, and bright, flowing clothes. Loretta easily picked up all the bookkeeping and management details that Iris was delighted to be rid of.

"Good morning," Iris greeted her.

Loretta barely looked up from her computer as Iris and Sheba passed by. "Back at you, boss. Do you need anything for your phone call with Mr. Harcon at 11:00? You don't want to keep that man waiting. I looked him up. That man's not just Maserati rich. He's moonshot rich!"

"Thanks, but I'm ready for him." Iris glanced around the still-bare reception area. "But why don't you go ahead and order those two visitor's chairs I chose the other day? Get them quick-shipped if you can. And we need to find some tasteful furniture for the conference room. We don't want moonshot-rich Alex Harcon sitting on the floor."

"On it. I'll find some pieces to add some color to this place. Maybe purple chairs." Loretta winked at her.

Iris and Sheba moved into the open-office bullpen which, admittedly, looked a bit monochromatic. A dozen black-and-white photographs of her past projects lined the tasteful gray walls. Several light wood flat files were grouped in a corner and a large, impressive model sat on a stand outside the door to the empty conference room.

Her new architect Rollo Baptiste was collecting black line drawings as they emerged from a new large-format printer. He had measured the house for their newest renovation project and converted the dimensions into detailed drawings of the existing conditions. Rollo gathered the prints together, rolled them up, and handed them to her. "The Brewster Street as-builts." He ran a hand through his short, curly, black hair. He was operating at slow speed these days, given that his wife had just had a baby.

Iris entered her private office and dumped the drawings on her drafting table. She sat at the desk and logged on to her computer to see if there were any urgent emails from clients. It was still hard for her to believe that she had employees depending on her for steady paychecks. What would happen to Rollo and Loretta if her workload fell off and she couldn't afford to keep them on? Architecture could be a brutally cyclical business.

At the moment however, Reid Associates was in good shape. The museum project, two house renovations, and a jewelry store fit-out were keeping them more than busy. But didn't every company need a financial cushion to tide them through the lean times?

Iris taped the print of the Brewster Street first floor plan flat onto her drafting table. She unrolled some tracing paper over it and began to sketch, eliminating a back staircase and sketching out a larger, more efficient kitchen.

She had almost completed the redesign when her phone rang. 11:00 already. Iris waited as Alex Harcon's P.A. put her through to him. She and Alex had worked together previously on a project and ended up sharing a dangerous adventure that left them on friendlier terms than most clients and architects. Not romantic, more like fellow war survivors.

Iris doodled while she waited on hold.

"Iris, hello. Are you ready for the Historic Commission meeting next Tuesday? You still certain I shouldn't be there?"

"I'm sure. They're going to ask a lot of technical questions and I know how to present the project so it sounds uncontroversial. We want to keep a low profile."

Iris was not really sure. These meetings were invariably a popularity contest, and the often-cranky commissioners disliked outsiders. A billionaire flying in from California to present a non-traditional design proposal for a building he'd bought in a prominent

Harvard Square location might raise their hackles. On the other hand, they might be swayed by his celebrity. Always hard to predict.

"But your design is modern. Don't these guys want all the buildings in the Square to look like they were built in the 19th century, if not the 18th?"

"Not necessarily. I'll make the design decisions sound justified from an aesthetic point of view. Most of the people on the panel are reasonable."

"Fine, I'll leave this in your capable hands. But they'd better let us build our project exactly as you've designed it. Let me know how it goes."

"I will."

Alex continued, "There's something else I'd like to run past you. An acquaintance of mine is a TV producer. He and I were discussing the museum, and he thought the story of its design and construction might make an interesting show for a streaming network. This project is a real labor of love for me, a showcase for all the art I've been collecting. I quite like the idea of having it documented—with your help of course, since you would have a central role in the film. Your firm and the contractor would get a lot of publicity. So would the museum."

Iris shuddered. "I'm not an actress. I get nervous when I have to speak in public."

"You did a great job speaking at the AIA Convention in April. Anyway, this guy, Glen Forester, wants to meet you. Will you at least hear his pitch? It would mean a lot to me. And, of course, you'd be getting a performance fee for each episode."

Iris hesitated. "Okay, Alex. I'll talk to Glen and listen to what he has in mind."

After she rang off, she sat staring at her phone. What had she just agreed to? And did she have a choice?

2

102 *Mount Auburn Street? Can't be.* Trent Westbrook sat in his suburban Weston sunroom on a bright Monday morning, eating breakfast while he read *The Boston Globe*. Alex Harcon was turning a Harvard Square building into a museum at 102 Mount Auburn Street? Trent tossed a half-eaten piece of toast toward his plate. It missed and landed on the tablecloth, buttered side down.

His wife Deirdra looked up from inspecting the front-page headlines and absently flipped the toast back onto the plate, shaking the crumbs from her fingers. "What's wrong, dear?"

Trent stroked his receding chin as if he was Abraham Lincoln, an old habit he knew Deirdra detested. "Nothing I can't handle." At least he hoped that was the case. The election for the Junior Senator's seat from Massachusetts was six weeks away and he couldn't let the slightest whiff of this story get out—or losing the election would be the least of his problems.

He staggered from the table. "I need to make some calls before I head in to Campaign HQ."

In his private home office, Trent sat down and opened a laptop on the mahogany desk. He thought for a few moments, considering his options. He wondered what Jimbo Dugan might be up to these days. He Googled his old school friend using his actual name.

Well, blow me away. The James Dugan he recognized, as opposed to the assortment of photos of seven other ones, was now a golf pro at The Country Club in Brookline, just a few miles away. That might be a useful connection. The guy must hear a lot of scuttlebutt from their exclusive membership. Maybe he should have kept Dugan on his Christmas card list. But was Jimbo still trustworthy, or should Trent pass this assignment along to his regular fixer? He debated, then decided Jimbo had as much at stake as Trent himself did, almost. He took a deep breath, fished a burner phone out of a locked drawer, and made the call.

"Jim Dugan here."

"Jiiiimbo. It's been a long time, old friend."

There were a few seconds of silence. "T-bone?"

"Ahhh, could be. No names, OK?"

"Yeah, I heard you were—"

"Exactly. I was just reading in *The Globe* about a new renovation being proposed at a certain address in Harvard Square."

There was a short pause. "Oh, shit!"

"Yeah. The project goes before the Historic Commission next Tuesday for some approval or other. I imagine we'd both like to know whether their plans involve tearing up the floor under the stairs."

Jimbo let out an anguished moan.

"Let's not panic yet. Why don't you go to the meeting on Tuesday night? It's open to the public. Find out what this architect, Iris Reid, is proposing to do to the building and see whether she gets it approved."

"Why can't *you* go?"

"Because people recognize me now. You can go incognito."

"I'm six-foot-five and 275 pounds. You think I won't stand out?"

"Scrunch down. Wear a big coat. It's important that we get some intel, so we know what we might need to do."

"*We?*"

"We both have a lot to lose. If Kegs were alive, I'm sure he'd want to be our advance guy."

"Yeah, but he's not, is he?"

3

The next morning, Iris tried to keep busy in her office as she waited for Glen Forester to arrive for his appointment. Through her interior office window, she could see across the workstations to the reception area and, at the stroke of 10:00, a tall man with tousled, bleached blond hair entered through the glass door. Iris studied him as he chatted with Loretta. He was around her age and wore a dark T-shirt under a faded black leather jacket with jeans. He didn't look too intimidating.

Iris crossed through the middle of the open workspace. Glen turned toward her and offered his hand. "Glen Forester, from Easy A Productions."

Iris walked him back to her office where he sat across from her in one of the visitor's chairs, scanning the photos of her past projects on the wall. Sheba warily sniffed the newcomer's boots, then curled up in her bed in the corner, keeping him in sight.

"Mr. Forester, Alex Harcon tells me you're interested in filming the construction of his new museum."

"Call me Glen, please. My idea is a bit more encompassing than that. I've been putting together creative content for a streaming channel called Roku. Do you know it?"

"Sorry, I don't watch much TV."

"No matter. I've been doing some original programming for them, like the *Charlie Chaplin* biopic." He looked at her expectantly for some sign of recognition.

"The one with Robert Downey Junior?

"Uh, no. Ours was a compilation of Chaplin's own film clips. We had twelve episodes, and it did super with the audience numbers. I also came up with the concept for *The Great Southern Baking Show*. That one's just been renewed for Season Six. Anyway, Roku has some patrons who are interested in more highbrow shows—like that river cruise line that sponsors so many of the PBS specials. The show I'm thinking of wouldn't be as intense as a Ken Burns film. It would be more accessible and dynamic than that, but let's say, cultured."

"Uh huh."

"When Mr. Harcon showed me his museum's media package, with the picture of you standing in front of those drawings of the proposed building, I had an inspiration: the Roku viewers follow the project from your initial sketches to the completed building. You talk about your design process, and we see you discussing and developing your concepts with Mr. Harcon. You know, there might be some conflicts here and there, and you could defend your vision. We'd also film the progress of construction once it starts. There's always some surprise or minor catastrophe that can make good TV. It would be sort of like 'This Old House-meets-a-PBS-documentary' with you in the starring role. Doesn't hurt that it's a woman-owned business."

Iris thought this was sounding way too focused on her. "I thought you wanted to document the museum's construction."

"We do. But we need an angle, more context to juice it up for the audience. They'll want to learn how you thought up the design. Get to know all the personalities involved in the whole process. You're the one who ties it together, and I bet you have an interesting back story. There can't be many female architects designing museums. And isn't your partner a chef who won a James Beard award? We could rope him in too."

"No, I'd like to leave my personal life out of this." Or would Luc consider this good publicity for the restaurant? His picture on the cover of Boston Magazine declaring him "the sexiest chef in New England" sure hadn't hurt business.

Glen flapped a hand. "We can discuss those details later. You would be paid a fee, of course. Maybe $5000. per episode? Plus, your firm and the contractor would get valuable publicity. Mr. Harcon would also get a lot of visibility for his new museum."

Iris reflected on the fact that Alex Harcon was giving her this incredible design opportunity. And he clearly wanted her to agree to this video business. How big a deal would it be to let Easy A Productions film her in action for brief periods? And Glen Forester, sitting across from her, had mentioned a performance fee. That could help pay for the new office furniture.

"Of course, we'd have to do a talent reel to sell the show to the streaming service. Then we'd shoot a pilot and go from there."

Iris tried to imagine herself in this role, sitting in a burgundy leather wingback chair like Alistair Cooke. It seemed absurd.

"I don't really think I have TV potential."

"I disagree. I think you'd have incredible charisma on the screen, TVQ we call it. And I can always spot it."

"Would there be a script?"

"Yes, and no. We'd go over ideas before each taping session. But there would be room for you to improvise. How about if I email you some details? You can think about it." Glen studied her expression. "And I might be able to negotiate you a higher performance fee."

"Okay," Iris said, more to get rid of Glen Forester than out of any actual interest. Bottom line: Alex Harcon wanted this, so she really didn't have much choice. With any luck, Iris could make some quick money to give her business a cushion and then leave hr short television career behind her.

After Glen left, Iris collected the gym bag she kept in a corner of her office holding her karate gi and brown belt. She'd slip out to an 11:30 sparring class. If she was going to be on TV, she needed to make sure she was in peak physical shape.

4

After lunch at her desk, Iris walked Sheba down Garden Street towards Harvard Square. When the two of them entered the Mass Avenue storefront, now under construction for a future jewelry store, the contractor, Milo, glanced up from his table saw. He turned off the power and slid his goggles onto the top of his head.

"Uh, oh. Architect's here. She's gonna change stuff," he said to no one in particular, since he was the only one in the small space.

"When have I ever made you change anything? And where's your crew?"

"Down at Charlie's Kitchen. And they'd better be bringing me back a veggie burger."

Milo was anything but your typical contractor. He moonlighted as a rock musician and wore tight black leather pants to his day job, even on a balmy September day like today. He tied his waist-length black hair in a ponytail to keep it from getting caught in the power tools. His crew looked like a local chapter of the Hell's Angels, and they were all devoted to their boss.

"How's it coming along?" This site visit was more a formality than actual supervision. Iris had complete confidence in Milo's finish carpentry skills and his willingness to follow her drawings.

"Have a look."

She walked over to the built-in mahogany niches that lined one wall. Reveals had been inscribed along three sides for glass shelves to slide into. "Very slick. Will you order the glass doors soon?"

"They'll come measure for them after I finish the niches on the other side, which should be in two more days. Everything's on schedule."

This was the third project Iris had worked on with Milo. She had been lucky enough to discover him when she'd desperately needed a contractor to renovate the decrepit building that became the *Paradise* restaurant. Milo had come through for her on a tight schedule and they'd developed a friendly working relationship since.

"Will you be ready to start on the museum next month?"

"Sure. When do you think you'll get the Historical Commission sign-off so I can pull the permit?"

Iris ran a hand along the smooth surface of the finely sanded cabinets. "The hearing is scheduled for Tuesday. If all goes well, they should write up the approval and you can apply for the permit right after that."

"Good timing. We should finish up here in three weeks."

"About the museum…"

Milo regarded her warily. "A problem? Don't tell me Harcon's having budgeting issues or wants to have his own builder do it."

"No. A TV producer approached me and asked if I'd allow him to film bits of the construction process to air on a streaming service."

Milo balanced back against a sawhorse and crossed his arms. "Like *This Old House?* Do I have to wear a plaid shirt and Dad pants?"

"No, you can wear a *Ritual Magic* T-shirt to advertise your band. And your contracting business would get tons of publicity as well, not that I want you to get too busy to work on my projects."

"Did you already say yes to the TV people?"

"Harcon really wants us to agree. This museum is his baby, and he wants it documented for all eternity."

"Wants *us* to agree. You mean *I* get a say?"

"I'm not sure that either of us can refuse."

"It could be a hassle if they get in my way or mess up the schedule." Milo cocked his head. "How do you feel about it?"

Iris hesitated. "It would be good PR for us. It shows we can handle prestigious projects."

"Unless there's some disaster on site and we screw up in front of thousands of people."

Iris couldn't tell if Milo was concerned or amused at the prospect.

5

Glen Forester called the next morning and suggested he shoot her talent reel in the loft. "We're not just selling you. We're selling your personality, your design sense. Plus, you'll feel more comfortable in your own space."

Iris didn't like the idea. She thought after she'd agreed to be filmed, it was a done deal. She didn't think she'd have to audition.

"I'll record you on my phone while I ask you some questions, okay? Very informal."

Later that afternoon, she sat across from Glen in her living room, Sheba next to her on the sofa. But Iris wore a red Gabriela Hearst pantsuit with shoulder pads and a nipped-in waist and had applied extra makeup because she'd heard that video washed out color. She'd even blown out her hair, so it fell in shiny waves to her shoulders. But she felt like a fraud. This wasn't her, all glammed up. She was more comfortable in jeans and work boots.

She and her boyfriend Luc shared this loft above his restaurant, the Paradise. Light poured into the room through five oversized windows. A modern, surfboard-shaped coffee table was in front of her, and a razor-etched Elliott Puckette painting hung on the wall behind.

Glen checked his light meter. "No need for overhead lights. Let's get started." He set his iPhone on a small tripod next to him and gripped a remote controller in his hand. "Why don't we begin with you telling me a little about yourself—how you got interested in architecture and how you started your firm."

Iris had practiced this part in front of a mirror. "My major in college was sculpture, and I wanted to find a profession that dealt with three-dimensional form but had some real impact on people's lives. After I apprenticed for a few years with a large New York firm, I came back to Cambridge where I'd gone to school and hung out a shingle. My firm specializes in residential work, but we gradually began taking on other kinds of buildings: restaurants, stores, art studios and now a museum."

"How did Alex Harcon first hear about you?"

"Ah. Last year, I was turning an old brick warehouse in Medford into several artists' studios for a showcase sponsored by *Architecturenow! Magazine*. I was soliciting green building products from various vendors when I read about the new Harcon solar roof system. I took the chance of contacting Alex Harcon to see if he wanted to test it out on our project. We were in the right place at the right time and the collaboration went well."

Glen nodded. "And that led to him offering you the museum commission?"

"Alex had seen photographs of some of my other work in magazines. Every project I design is different, based on the client's needs and site conditions. You can tell a lot about an architect's sensibility from their work. And Alex and I had already developed a working relationship during the construction of the studio showcase." Iris left out the part where they'd bonded over their desperate search for a terrifying high-tech weapon that had been stolen from Alex.

"Was there a competition involved for the museum?"

"Alex asked me to submit design ideas for the site. I showed him some sketches and described how I thought the space could work with his art collection. It turned out that we were on the same wavelength, so he hired me for the commission. Again, the stars aligned."

Glen clicked off the remote. "That was great. Very polished." He scrolled briefly through the video. "And I can tell the camera likes your face. I'll make my presentation to the network tomorrow. Assuming they give us the green light, I'll call you about the next steps."

After Glen left, Iris realized she actually wanted this job. It might be fun.

6

On Tuesday night, Iris arranged to meet Rollo at the Historic Commission meeting at 6:00. He would bring the slides he'd taken of the buildings in Harvard Square with design features similar to those they were proposing. *Similar* being a relative term.

Iris was an active, local architect. The eight Commissioners knew her, and she knew them. She was familiar with which ones liked to hear themselves talk, whether on topic or not. Some were sticklers for weaving new buildings into a conservative relationship with their neighbors, and some were willing to champion a more modern interpretation, if it was well-designed.

She'd try to convince the Commissioners that the stepping vertical planes of her design were reminiscent of nearby bay windows, and the materials proposed—glass, copper, wood and a vertical wall of greenery—could all be found on neighboring buildings. No need to mention that the wood cladding would be charred black in the Japanese shou sugi ban method. And she'd be sure to show an unappealing picture of the ugly office building they were replacing, purposely taken on a depressing, rainy day.

She'd submitted their application early in the month, hoping to avoid a late-night review slot when the Commissioners were tired. Some of those meetings dragged on until midnight. At 6:00 on the dot, Iris found Rollo outside the conference room, scanning the evening's posted agenda.

"Where are we in the line-up?" Iris asked.

"Nine applications. We're third. After the Turtle issue."

"Damn. That one could take forever with all the protesters."

Sometimes the Commission scheduled a controversial application for early in the evening to get it over with and thin out the audience as soon as possible. From the size of the crowd filling the room, there would be a big response to the Turtle application, no doubt a heated one.

Iris and Rollo took their seats in the second row. He had worn a coat and tie for the occasion, and she'd worn a tweed jacket to blend in with the Commissioners' ivy-league style.

The first submission went quickly. An earnest young architect made a case for why his client needed to add an egress window to a basement for fire safety. After the Commissioners deliberated over the width of the dividing mullions in the new basement window, insisting on the more historic single-pane glass with skinny mullions, it was approved.

Iris was cautiously optimistic. Sometimes a positive attitude in the room lingered on. Other times, the Commissioners felt a need to take a corrective stand to prove they were not pushovers.

When the secretary read out the second case number, the air in the room became charged. The Turtle was a beloved sandwich shop on Brattle Street in Harvard Square. Generations of Cantabrigians and Harvard students had Proustian memories of its hand-sliced Pastrami Reubens and comforting tuna melts. Long-time owner Abe Golden had died, and his widow sold the tiny two-story building to a developer who wanted to demolish it and build a new edifice eight stories tall. Even though the quirky, original structure was nothing special, the townspeople wanted to protect the few remaining unique buildings in the Square. The protesters were all ages and looked like they'd come prepared for battle. Maybe the Turtle's famous sandwiches would be gone, but its funky little building might still be saved from the wrecking ball.

The secretary proceeded to read out the developer's written proposal. The developer himself had not shown up but had sent his lawyer, who looked like he wanted to be anywhere but in this room. He carefully answered a few of the Commissioners' questions and then the meeting was opened to public comments. Forty people lined up to speak their minds. Iris exchanged an exasperated look with Rollo and glanced at the wall clock. The first speaker unwound a long story about how her husband had proposed to her in the Turtle. More followed.

More than an hour later, the public comment period was declared over. Iris was amazed that only three speakers had been escorted out of the room, shouting and using profanity. In the end, the Commissioners predictably tabled the proposal for further study, preferably by some other bureaucracy like the Harvard Square Conservation District. They ordered a ten-minute break so the remaining partisans in the audience could clear out of the room, with much grumbling, no one particularly happy.

The remaining few seemed like locals who showed up for these meetings regularly, viewing them as free evening entertainment, or other applicants patiently waiting for their turns. One elderly woman in the front row sat placidly knitting throughout the impassioned defenses for the Turtle, though the poor dear may have simply been deaf. Iris couldn't help thinking of Dickens' Madame Defarge knitting next to the guillotine during the French Revolution. She also noticed a large middle-aged man in a raincoat who was slouching down in his seat at the other end of the second row. He looked nervous, possibly about his own upcoming proposal.

When the Commissioners filed back into the room and retook their seats, the secretary read out the application number for Iris's project. She and Rollo rose and carried the four foam-core boards with their mounted color renderings to the Commissioners' table and took their seats facing them.

After the secretary read out the proposal itself, showing the Commission staff's own slides of the existing building and the drawings that Iris had submitted, Iris and Rollo stood up, identifying themselves for the record. Rollo fiddled with his laptop until his first image appeared on a screen at the end of the table as Iris propped up her sketches on the easels provided. Then she presented her case, studying the faces of the Commissioners as she spoke to gauge their reactions. Rollo advanced the slides to illustrate her points.

During the question-and-answer period, the first person to lift his finger to speak was, predictably, the Commissioner who liked the sound of his own voice. "I'm unconvinced that this modern façade will fit into the fabric of the Square." The blowhard proceeded to niggle about individual design features, arguing they differed too much from the surrounding buildings. Before Iris could launch into a defense, the Commissioner who liked modern buildings spoke up. "Fergus, nothing built in the 21st century is going to match Georgian architecture regardless, so why not create something new that plays nicely with the neighbors instead of trying to mimic them? This isn't Williamsburg."

The argument went back and forth a few rounds with the other Commissioners watching, to see who backed down first. Iris's advocate got in the last word. "I applaud the way this design matches the scale and general materials of the other buildings on the block. I support approval with no modifications." Several of the other men nodded their heads.

When Iris finished answering questions, they all stood and approached the sketches for a closer look. Iris looked over at Rollo and he gave her an encouraging smile.

Her design proposal passed 7-1.

7

Early the next morning, Iris emailed Alex with the good news about the approval but didn't expect to hear back from him until a reasonable hour, California time.

Getting an approval on the first go-round from the Historic Commission for a modernist design was a big deal, and she wanted to celebrate. She and Rollo had stopped at the Cantab Lounge after the meeting for a quick drink, but he'd had to get home to his wife and baby.

Iris called her friend, Ellie, who always welcomed an opportunity to procrastinate from writing her book on Milanese architecture of the 1920's. Ten minutes later, Ellie sailed through the front door of Reid Associates.

Through the interior windows of her office, Iris watched Ellie exchange remarks with Loretta and both women laughed. Ellie waved to Rollo as she waltzed through the open bullpen back to Iris's office. She shut the door behind her and lowered the interior window blinds.

"What are you doing?" Iris asked. "Why do we need privacy?"

Ellie pulled a bottle of Dom Perignon out of her tote bag and set it on Iris's desk.

"At 9:30 in the morning?" Iris reached over to confirm that the bottle was chilled.

"Why not? We're celebrating." Ellie continued unpacking two crystal flutes from their bubble wrap cocoons and peeled off the bottle's foil top. "We can find some o.j. somewhere if pure champy in the morning is too decadent for you."

Iris held up her glass for Ellie to fill. "And adulterate Dom?"

"It's from a patient of Mack's." A loud pop erupted before Ellie reached out quickly and caught the cork in the air. "I was waiting for an occasion to open it."

After they'd downed a glass each, Ellie wanted to hear all the details about the previous night's meeting. Iris filled her in while they worked their way through the rest of the bottle.

"Too bad those lily-livered Commissioners didn't grow spines and veto the developer's plan to demolish the Turtle. I loved their Reubens!"

Iris was starting to feel loopy. "I'm just glad our approval went through because this TV producer wants to start filming soon."

"You agreed to it?"

Iris rubbed her temples lightly. "I'm not sure I had a choice. Alex really wanted it."

Ellie sighed. "These billionaires and their vanity projects."

"But I got to design a museum due to Alex's vanity, so I'm not complaining. Being in this film is a small price to pay. And speaking of payments, the producer said I'd earn $6000. per episode. That will help with my finances."

"Are you having cash-flow issues? Is it the start-up expenses for this great new office? Nice chairs in the reception area, by the way. But I thought the museum fee was covering all that."

"I just want to make sure that I can keep making payroll in case work ever dries up."

"Such is the burden of being a business owner. Not that I'd know about that."

"I'll feel more comfortable if I can put aside some savings. Plus, the filming will be good marketing for bringing in more work."

"True enough. But let's talk about the really important part of your new TV career. What are you going to wear?"

8

Trent agreed to Jimbo's suggestion to meet in the Chestnut Hill Mall parking lot on Route 9, a busy location convenient to his golf pro job. He could afford to allow Jimbo a small power move.

At precisely noon, an old Subaru hatchback pulled up alongside his immense Lincoln Navigator and Jimbo got out. While he slowly ambled around toward the Lincoln, Trent made some observations. His high school buddy walked in a way that suggested his chinos and light jacket were a little too tight. An okay look for a country club golf pro, and it showed that he obviously wasn't packing. His facial expression had changed from dumb high-school jock to defeated middle-aged loser. Trent shuddered. They hadn't even hit forty yet, but this guy had his future written all over him.

"Jimbo!" He greeted the man sliding into the passenger seat. "Long time."

"It's *Jim* now, T-bone. Nice little car."

Trent's campaign manager had advised him to leave his non-US-made Mercedes S500 stashed in the garage until after the election, but at least the Lincoln had the darkest tinted windows the state allowed, and he didn't have one of those show-offy license plates to broadcast his identity.

"So," Trent began, "let's brainstorm about the 102 Mount Auburn Street situation. You said the architect specified marble floors. That doesn't really clarify our options. They could keep the subfloor intact or rip it up and replace it."

"The architect didn't go into details like that. The meeting was mainly about what it would look like from the outside. I went up to look at the drawings afterward and saw the note about the marble. Oh, yeah, and she's moving the staircase."

"OK. Well done." Trent massaged his chin. "I think we have to assume the worst. We need to get in there and remove the package."

"Remove the package." Jimbo repeated slowly. "Just how do we do that?"

"There's probably not much left at this point, mainly dust. I think I remember that the floor had some kind of vinyl tiles. You could pry them up with a crowbar, flip up a few floorboards, stuff the plastic bag in your duffle, pack it all back down, and walk away. I can get rid of what's inside the duffle. And then our problem will be gone for good."

Jimbo regarded him warily. "And who draws the short straw and gets to break in, or are *we* going in as a team, like last time?"

"If you'll do the honors on site, I can make the remains disappear. Does that sound like a fair exchange?"

"Not really." Jimbo looked truculent. "You dragged Kegs and me into this thing twenty years ago. Like idiots, we followed you. And now you want me to take all the risk and clean up your mess. Jeez, do you think I'm that stupid? You're the one who'd be in truly deep shit if this ever came to light. To say the least, you'd never hold a political office again."

Trent blew out a breath. "You're not a blameless Boy Scout here. I remember what you and Kegs did to the guy."

"As you told us to do. We were just stupid kids, and you played us."

Trent placed his hands carefully on top of the steering wheel. "Jimbo. Or rather, Jim. I agree that you would have the riskier role to play here. How about this? I pay you $10,000. for wrapping this up successfully. Does that sound better?"

"Twenty."

Trent studied Jimbo's face. Ah, well—the amount didn't matter. He'd eliminate this loose end the same way he had with poor old Kegs. "Deal."

9

It was mid-October, prime foliage season in Massachusetts. Iris and Loretta stood looking out the windows along the front of the office. The leaves on the trees lining both sides of the street looked like they were on fire in the bright sunlight.

Iris checked her watch. "She's cutting it close."

"She'll be here," Loretta assured her.

"I can't believe Ellie talked me into this. It seems…unprofessional."

Loretta shrugged. "Fake it 'til you make it."

Glen's camera crew was scheduled to arrive in half an hour to film the pilot. As arranged, Iris would discuss how she'd started her firm and how she had met Alex Harcon. Ellie had volunteered to come in and sit at one of the empty desks in the bullpen to fill out the office shots and make Reid Associates appear to be a larger enterprise.

When a blue Volvo station wagon pulled into the driveway a few minutes later, there were two figures in the front seat.

"Raven was home and wanted to come too." Ellie announced as she entered with a tall, beautiful young woman with short, spiky black hair and huge brown eyes. "You have three desks, don't you?" Ellie looked over at the office manager. "Loretta, this is my daughter, Iris's goddaughter." Ellie mock whispered to Raven, "Loretta really runs this place."

Hugs were exchanged all around. Iris regarded Raven, dressed in a dark gray suit. "I've never seen you looking so corporate."

"This is my outfit for grant interviews and funerals." Raven was a painter in her last year at the Rhode Island School of Design, in Providence. She usually had a vivid accent streak in her hair, a different color each time Iris saw her. "Mom said to tone it down and try to look like an architect. Do I pass?"

Iris gestured at her own suit, the same one that she'd worn for her talent reel. "We're usually in jeans and work boots when we're not meeting with clients."

"I brought my laptop and can pretend that I'm designing something. Where should I sit?"

Rollo looked up from his desk in the open office with interest when he noticed Raven. "Need help rearranging the desks?"

He, Loretta and Raven moved the furniture around and piled up blackline prints and catalogs on all the surfaces until it looked like three busy architects worked there. Rollo put some of his sketches and several rolls of tracing paper on Raven's desk. Ellie and Raven took their seats, opened their laptops, and tried to look busy. Iris instructed them not to stare into the camera and, if possible, to avoid saying anything.

Loretta made her way to the neatly organized kitchenette in one corner, a study in right angles, and made a new pot of coffee. She placed a mug on each desk.

Iris checked her makeup. Did she have lipstick on her teeth? Through her exterior window, she spotted two vans and Glen's BMW pulling into the parking spaces behind the office. She rose to greet the team.

Glen entered first, accompanied by a slight, middle-aged man with combed back hair and a prominent forehead. "This is the showrunner I told you about, Nili Peretz." Iris shook his outstretched hand. Evidently this guy was a big deal, according to Glen. Nili proceeded to walk around the office, his eyes slowly panning from side to side.

Five other people crowded into the reception area, and Glen continued the introductions, but Iris forgot most of the names instantly.

The director of photography, James, was a skinny guy with wire-rimmed glasses and a flat newsboy cap which gave him a Bolshevik look. He seemed to be openly sizing her up, maybe evaluating her TVQ.

The sound person, a short woman with heavy black glasses, wore a long-suffering expression and carried a pile of blankets. "The gaffer's still in the van getting his lighting gear."

Glen reappeared at Iris's side. "You won't see much of the media manager. She's mainly in the van or the studio working behind the scenes, shaping the content."

Iris wondered at the way these people spoke. *Shaping the content.* It was like learning a new language.

Loretta ushered people back to the conference room as soon as Iris met them.

Two women remained in the doorway. A mousy young woman was introduced as an assistant. "I can run out to get coffee and lunches or anything else you need," she stated. And Tonya, a zaftig blond on the early side of middle-age, was in charge of hair and make-up. Tonya approached Iris and stared at her face. "The camera's gonna love you. That bone structure, that porcelain skin. I'll add a bit of color for today. We don't want you looking washed out."

Just when Iris thought she'd met everyone, a crazy-looking mountain man pushed through the glass doors. His hair and beard merged into a platinum jungle. He carried several reflectors under one arm and guided an aluminum suitcase on wheels. "And this is our gaffer," Glen said. "He's in charge of lighting."

Iris rubbed the back of her neck. Had she invited in a circus?

With nine people bustling around the conference room, each fiddling with the mysterious paraphernalia of their spheres of expertise, the space felt to Iris like it had shrunk. Glen huddled with Nili, the showrunner, and James, the director of photography, studying two monitors attached to a complicated camera with a very long lens.

"Wheels or stationery?"

"Wheels. Let's capture Iris's face from several angles."

Nili wandered over to where Iris sat with a plastic cape around her shoulders, while Tonya applied highlighter to her cheeks and chin.

"Pucker your lips, hon." Tonya instructed Iris and demonstrated with her own mouth while brandishing a bright red lipstick.

"I don't usually wear such a dark color," Iris protested.

"Trust me. The camera will make this look like clear lip gloss."

Nili studied her from different sides, then returned to Glen and James, saying something to them sotto voce. Iris felt like a specimen under a microscope.

The media manager was seated nearby, peering at the screens. Her contribution was, "We don't want to make the viewer dizzy, James, but I suppose I can fix that in editing."

The assistant appeared at Iris's side with what looked like a large laptop. She set it on the table and flipped open the lid. "We put the text you worked out with Glen on a teleprompter. I'll set this up near the camera."

"I don't think I'll need that," Iris said. "Glen's going to feed me questions and I've pretty much memorized my answers."

"You might want to have it there in case you freeze up. It happens."

Would Iris forget her lines and make a fool of herself in front of all these people? She could see Loretta, Ellie, Raven, and Rollo all shooting interested glances into the conference room through the window to the bullpen. They'd be watching her performance, as well.

A loud metallic clank broke through her thoughts. A white

reflective umbrella on a tall stand had toppled over, and Mountain Man hurried to set it upright.

"Dammit, Sal. You trying to deafen me?" The sound woman pulled large earphones away from her ears. She'd spread out baffling and blankets on the floor in each corner to absorb extraneous sound and was checking the results. "Too many hard surfaces in here," she muttered.

The others ignored her. Nili led Iris to a certain seat, positioning her just so. Mountain man adjusted his panel lighting and reflectors. The assistant clipped a mic to Iris's lapel, and Tonya patted down some stray hairs.

Glen sat across from her, out of view of the camera. He began with the same set of questions he'd asked for the talent reel and Iris answered as they had discussed, trying to make her words sound spontaneous. They went through all of Glen's questions. Iris needed to reshoot two sections where she'd forgotten to breathe, and her voice had started to get squeaky.

After an hour and a half, Nili announced, "Great. That's a wrap. I want to get some shots walking around your office, chatting with some of your employees. Maybe that attractive young lady with the short hair?"

10

Iris nailed on a professional smile. "That's Raven, our intern. You might prefer to talk to Rollo, my architectural job captain. He's working on the museum project with me."

"Let's chat with all four of them. The media manager can decide later who to use once she's in the editing room."

The ungainly entourage collected its equipment and migrated into the central bullpen. The assistant passed out liability waivers for the four to sign. Iris and Ellie exchanged panicked looks, and Iris read the form over Ellie's shoulder, searching for a clause that might pick up the imposters.

Tonya flurried around, adding a layer of make-up to the women's faces. Loretta's cornrows were magenta today, so Tonya gave her a matching lip shade.

Rollo tried to run a comb through his short, curly black hair, but Tonya fluffed it back out. "It looks better with some volume, hon."

Nili decided to have Glen interview Ellie first. The two men discussed the sequence of questions while James set up his camera. The gaffer fiddled with the lighting and the sound woman had Ellie do a mic check. Rollo had placed a few of his early framing drawings for the museum on Ellie's desk. Iris hoped Glen wouldn't ask her friend any technical questions about them.

James called, "Go." And Glen quickly consulted his notes. "Ellie MacKenzie, how long have you been with Reid Associates?"

"Gee, it feels like we've been working together forever, but it hasn't actually been that long. Iris makes work fun and we all feel valued as a team."

"Do you think that has anything to do with this being a woman-run office?"

"You mean, are women more collaborative than men? That's a bit of a generalization. I know that Iris welcomes our input, but I don't know if it's fair to say that it's gender specific."

Iris shifted in her chair. Was Ellie purposely avoiding anything too soundbite-friendly so the media manager wouldn't use her segment?

Nili was frowning. He rested a hand on Glen's shoulder.

"Well, thank you, Ellie. Food for thought." Glen moved quickly over to Rocco's desk and James repositioned the camera. "So, I understand you are Rocco Baptiste, and you're the job captain for the museum project that will be under construction soon."

"Yes, our contractor is set to break ground tomorrow." Rocco sat rigidly in his chair, gripping his armrest. "We're very excited."

"What's been your contribution to the job?'

"I've been involved in the design development phase and producing structural drawings. I also built the model." Rollo moved toward a table holding a detailed replica of the museum.

James tried to follow behind at a steady speed on the dolly and rolled in for a close-up of the model, panning the camera from above down to a lower perspective.

Rollo lifted off the miniature glass solar tile roof to reveal the triple height atrium, with its multiple overhanging balconies. A wall of greenery lined one side of the atrium and was echoed as part of the street-side façade. Thin panels of copper and blackened wood featured on the Cubist-inspired front view.

"What will your role be during construction?" Glen asked.

"Iris and I will share responsibilities during the supervision phase. She's worked with our contractor before and trusts that he'll build according to our drawings and specifications. But it's still the architect's job to verify that and to review the contractor's invoices with the client." Rocco was looking more relaxed and using his hands now to gesture.

"Cut." James called out. "Great. Love the model." He turned to the media manager. "I'd like to use that shot in the opening credits." She nodded and noted it on her phone.

"Okay. Who's next?" Nili asked. "We've still got the office manager and the intern to do. Let's go with the office manager next. Loretta, right? We should have you sitting at the front desk."

The crew set up their gear in the reception area. As before, Glen stood to the side of the camera to direct his questions from out of sight.

"Loretta Jackson, good morning. How long have you been the office manager here at Reid Associates?"

Loretta rolled her eyes toward the ceiling in concentration. "Just over two months now."

"And what do you like best about working here?"

"I have a lot of responsibility. I do the bookkeeping and keep everyone on schedule. If anything breaks down," she looked meaningfully at the large printer in the corner, "I need to call in someone to fix it. I make sure we have supplies. Lately, I've been ordering office furniture. It's a million little details." Loretta's bracelets jangled as she waggled her fingers. "But I keep the place running so the architects can do their jobs."

"Sounds like a lot of teamwork going on here at Reid Associates," Glen concluded.

"Absolutely. Iris is a great boss."

After James signaled the end to the segment, everyone turned to look at Raven. She was standing next to the model. "Want me to stay here or sit at my desk?" she asked.

Iris was not altogether comfortable about what Raven might say. Why had she let Ellie talk her into letting them impersonate employees?

"That's good by the model," James called out. "Lighting's perfect." The crew reassembled.

"Now, Raven," Glen said. "You're an intern here. What have you been working on?"

Raven glanced down. "I've been helping Rollo build this model, finding different materials for it. See these trees along the sidewalk? I made those. It's been really fun. Like building a dollhouse."

Ellie raised an eyebrow at Iris. Rollo's mouth hung open.

"How about this charred wood paneling? Were you the one who got that effect? How did you do it?"

"Well, I had to experiment a lot." Raven cocked her head. She looked so photogenic that Iris was certain they would feature her vignette. "It was tricky. I finally got the look Iris wanted by scorching basswood with a little propane torch—the kind they use in restaurants."

Iris remembered Luc showing Raven how to use a torch to caramelize sugar on top of crème brûlée. Her goddaughter was quite the actress.

"Really?" Glen sounded dubious. "How ingenious."

"That's a wrap," James announced. "I think we got some good footage here."

Glen turned to Iris. "We'll assemble this in the editing room with the media manager, then submit it to Roku as a pilot. They should get back to us right away. Assuming it's a go, we'll want to meet the contractor and film the start of the actual construction next week. Harcon's flying out for that, right?"

"He wouldn't miss it."

11

Jim Dugan reached up and took his tool kit down from the shelf in the hall closet of his condo. Since his divorce the previous year, he no longer had a basement with a full workshop and only had a small selection of tools at hand. What could he use to get the tile and floorboards up? He lifted out the upper tier of the box and studied his options. The hammer was a serious weight and size, but the pry bar was puny, way too small for the job. He needed the hefty crowbar still in his ex's basement. Was it worth the aggravation of dealing with her, or should he just go to Home Depot and buy a new one?

Jim couldn't believe he'd agreed to this. He'd been procrastinating, hoping that Trent would change his mind. And then it was his week with Jimmy Junior, so nothing was going to interfere with that. Now he actually had to make a plan. That friggin' Trent Westbrook, a complete and total asshole. Just like high school—still pulling his strings, making him do the grunt work. He wished he could talk to Kegs about his present predicament, but that option was gone. Boating accident, my ass. Kegs was a damn fine sailor. No way he would have hit those rocks, been thrown overboard, and drowned.

Did good old Trent have something to do with it? Jim wouldn't put it past the guy. After all, Jim and Kegs were the only ones, other than Trent himself, who knew what went down that night. But then, why hadn't Trent come after Jim?

And now, twenty years later, Trent expected Jim to get that poor kid's remains out of their hiding place before someone discovered them.

In the end, Jim went to a hardware store several towns away and paid in cash for a large crowbar. As usual, he'd left things until the last minute. Construction of the museum was about to start, so he needed to take care of this tonight. He was in his kitchen at dinnertime, but his stomach was too agitated to eat anything, though he did manage to down a few beers. To kill time, he watched an old Jack Ryan movie on his laptop. At midnight, Jim drank two cups of coffee to wake himself up. Afterward, he worried he'd have to use a restroom somewhere and get remembered or leave DNA behind. He was really bad at this.

It was 1:30 a.m. by the time Jim plodded out to his Subaru to start the mission. It occurred to him that using his own car might be a mistake, but screw it, he didn't have time to figure out another plan. Parking could also be a problem. Wasn't that how a lot of criminals got caught? By something stupid like a parking ticket? Not that he was a criminal.

Half an hour later, he parked in a lot on the east side of Harvard Square and slung his heavy duffle bag over his shoulder. As he walked, he eased the hood of his sweatshirt forward to keep his face in shadow.

Jim expected that the late hour would minimize the chance of anyone noticing him fumbling with Trent's old key to get into the building. When the door actually swung open, he blessed the cheap owners who hadn't bothered to change the lock over the many years.

He didn't want to have to attempt the credit card technique that he'd only watched demonstrated twice on the internet.

Jim heard no sounds inside and found his way by flashlight to the big open area with the staircase. Being in this space again brought back his old nightmares. But this time, there was construction gear all around the central room, and a pile of rumpled up green material in the corner. Jim retrieved the crowbar from his duffle bag and headed toward the open stairs.

That's when things went sideways. The green pile began to move. At first, Jim thought he'd imagined it. But he watched and a man who looked like a red-headed lumberjack emerged from underneath it. He had something in his hand and came charging straight at Jim with his head down, making a war-cry like he was Mel Gibson in *Braveheart*. He didn't have time to think about it. He just reacted, bringing up the crowbar to protect himself, to ward off the attack. The guy and the bar collided with far more force than Jim meant to use. There had been a crunch, the reverberation running up his arm.

The lumberjack fell to the ground, blood gushing from his forehead. As he fell forward, he managed to graze Jim's knuckles with the object in his hand, which turned out to be a large flashlight. Jim looked down at the man's profile and his blank, stunned expression. Screw this! Jim gathered up his bag and hightailed it out of there as quickly as he could, leaving the front door swinging open behind him.

Unbelievable! Jim should have known that anything associated with Trent Westbrook would be cursed. It was now 3 o'clock in the morning. He sat at the tiny kitchen table in his condo, examining his grazed knuckles and trying to get his trembling nerves in check. The adrenaline in his system continued to pump, now fueling anger. Why was that guy on a construction site in the middle of the night? Was he supposed to be like a watchdog? And, most important, had Jim killed him? Blood was leaking out the front of the guy's head. It looked bad. Frigging hell. The old nightmare was replaying itself.

Jim tried to make some sense of the order of events.

So, even though Jim had a key, the police could accuse him of breaking into a building, attacking an unarmed man with a crowbar, and possibly killing him. And he might have left a fingerprint, hair, or some other bit of evidence behind. But Jim had never been arrested, so he wouldn't be in their system. One thing he was sure of, if the police ever picked up Jim's trail, Trent would deny that he'd spoken to Jim since high school graduation.

Other than that other night twenty years before, Jim had been a law-abiding guy with a steady job. He tried to set a good example and teach Jimmy Junior the difference between right and wrong. Now, if the police somehow identified him as tonight's assailant, he might spend a major part of Jimmy's life locked up away from him.

Jim got up to find some antibiotic ointment to put on his knuckles. Could he get away with wearing golf gloves at work until this healed? Maybe he'd get lucky, and nothing would point the police in his direction.

But, at the end of the day, the plastic bag of remains he was supposed to remove was still there under the floorboards, so maybe the cops were the least of his worries. How could he get Trent off his back? Maybe he could claim that he had dug out those old bones and tossed them in the Charles River. Would Trent believe him?

12

Iris fumbled across the bedside table for her buzzing phone. 5:00 a.m.? She bolted upright on her side of the bed and hit Accept.

"It's Milo. I'm at Mt. Auburn Hospital with one of my workers. Carl got attacked late last night at the museum construction site." Milo's voice cracked. "He's in surgery now."

"Wait. Last night? I don't understand. What was he doing there at night?"

"His old lady kicked him out again, and he didn't know where else to go. I know, I'm pissed off too, but this isn't the time to go into it. I'm waiting for someone to tell me how the surgery went. Just thought you should know."

Iris was already scrambling into her clothes when Luc rolled over, looking at her questioningly, blinking away sleep.

"I'm coming there now," Iris said and hit End.

Luc propped himself up on an elbow, his hair rumpled. "What's going on?"

"One of the carpenters was attacked last night at the museum site. I'm going to Mt. Auburn Hospital to check on him and see if I can find out what happened."

"He was there at night?"

"He shouldn't have been." She leaned down to kiss him. "Go back to sleep. I'll call you when I know more."

Iris found Milo pacing around the otherwise-empty waiting room in the Surgical Center. Two empty coffee cups and his motorcycle helmet sat near a pile of ancient magazines on an end table.

"Any word?" Iris asked.

Milo spun around toward her. "You didn't have to come."

"I wanted to. Tell me what happened."

"I talked to Carl about two hours ago, when they were wheeling him into surgery. He was pretty out of it. I'd given him a key to the jobsite this afternoon when we moved in our tools. After Gail kicked him out, he couldn't think of anywhere else to go. He brought in a sleeping bag from his truck and was in that alcove under the stairs when he heard someone coming in the front door. He figured it was someone looking to steal something. He looked around for a weapon, but our tools were locked up. All Carl had was a heavy flashlight. Turns out the intruder had a crowbar."

"Oh, my God!"

"Carl tried to wrestle with the guy, but he got whacked in the forehead. He was barely able to dial 911 before he passed out and that's all he remembers. An ambulance brought him here. The poor bastard's been going in and out of consciousness. He told the hospital to call me during one of his lucid moments."

Iris expelled a long breath. "What have the doctors said?"

"That he has a serious concussion at the least, and they're worried about potential brain damage."

"Oh, no."

They sat down on a sofa in stunned silence. Finally, Iris said, "Why would anyone want to break into our construction site?"

Twenty minutes later, a distraught-looking woman with tanning-bed skin and smeared mascara pushed through the waiting room door.

Milo stood up. "Gail, he's still in surgery."

"What the hell happened, Milo? Some stranger broke into the construction site and hit Carl over the head with a crowbar? Why?"

"I don't know. That's all he could tell me before they wheeled him off. It's been two hours now. The doctor should be out any minute to give us a report."

Milo tipped his head toward Iris. "This is our architect, Iris Reid. She's concerned too."

Gail gave her a once-over and a curt nod.

Iris wondered about this woman who had thrown Carl out of the house earlier.

They waited a few more minutes in awkward silence before a door at the end of the hall swung open and a man in scrubs walked toward them. "Family of Carl Nowak?"

Gail rushed forward. "I'm his wife."

Milo and Iris followed at a slight distance. Iris couldn't stop staring at the spray of blood on the doctor's shoulder.

"The doctor introduced himself to Gail. I'm the neurosurgeon who operated on your husband. We were able to relieve the swelling in his brain caused by the skull fracture. Mr. Nowak is in recovery now. It's too early to tell the full extent of any brain damage that might have occurred."

Gail started to wobble, and Milo held her elbow to steady her.

"The CT scans look hopeful," the doctor continued, "but we won't know the repercussions from the intracranial bleeding for a while. These sorts of injuries take some time to stabilize. The ambulance paramedics did a tremendous job. They probably saved his life."

Gail let out a strangled sob. "When can I see him?"

"He'll be coming out of the anesthesia in about an hour, then we'll take him to the ICU and you can visit him there. He won't be able to talk because he'll have a tube in his throat. We should be able to remove that in a few days, then we'll need to monitor him for at least a week. He may have to spend some time in rehab, depending on what abilities have been compromised. Now, if you'll excuse me." He turned and disappeared through the swinging door.

Milo helped Gail back to a seat in the waiting room. "He's going to be all right. Carl is a fighter. You know how hard-headed the guy is." He took her hands in his. "And we're going to find the bastard who did this to him."

13

The breaking dawn cast the museum's façade in a grayish-pink haze. Iris and Milo stood on the sidewalk, peering carefully at the front door.

Milo aimed the beam of his phone's flashlight on the lock. "It doesn't look like anyone broke in."

"The intruder could have used lock picks, I guess. Did we ever change the cylinders after Alex took over the building?"

"Was I supposed to? I just use whatever key the client gives me. I haven't had a chance to set up new keys and a lockbox."

"This was an office building for the last fifty years. Who knows how many keys there are out there?"

"As soon as Bayside Locksmith opens up, I'll replace all the locks." Milo typed a note into his phone.

Iris fished out a jangling key ring from her purse and scanned the area. "I don't see any caution tape, so I guess we can go in."

"The cops, as well as the EMTs, and the ambulance would have responded to Carl's 911 call. I assume they dusted the door." Milo followed her in and flicked on the overhead lights. "The guy's fingerprints could be on file."

"We need to talk to the Cambridge police who are investigating this." Iris said. "Maybe they'll share what, if anything, they were able to learn."

At first glance, the central atrium looked relatively undisturbed. There was a layer of dust on pretty much every surface. Footprints from the EMTs and police officers' shoes showed tracks in the dust. Milo hadn't bothered to put down any floor protection, since the old vinyl tile would be torn up later. The lock on Milo's steel job site chest containing his tools was still latched. A rumpled green sleeping bag lay in an alcove under the staircase and a large flashlight was in a corner nearby.

"Do you see the weapon?" Iris asked. "It was a crowbar, right?"

"If it was left behind, the cops probably took it. But it wouldn't surprise me if the guy wore gloves."

"You think it was a professional? Not a homeless person on crack or off his meds? I doubt whoever it was expected to encounter anyone at night on a job site. So, what was the crowbar for? To pry something open? That rules out a homeless person looking for a quiet place to sleep."

"Maybe he was looking to steal some copper wiring from the basement."

"Well, he picked the wrong property. This building was constructed with cheap 1970s materials—thin sheetrock, aluminum electrical wiring, and mostly PVC plumbing pipes."

Iris and Milo made a tour of the other levels but found no signs of anything out of place. As they descended the stairs back to the first floor, Milo pointed to a spot near the tool chest. "Check that out." From this angle, they could make out a confusion of footprints looking as if a scuffle had occurred there.

Iris came closer and squatted down. "Is this blood?"

"Looks like it. It must be where Carl got hit."

Iris let that image recede. "I wonder if the thief figured Carl was dead? If so, wouldn't he have continued looking for whatever he was after?"

"Maybe he realized that there was nothing here worth stealing and moved on before Carl came to."

"We need to find out if there were other break-ins in the neighborhood last night."

"Harcon's not going to like the idea of a burglary attempt at a building that will house his valuable art collection."

Iris groaned. "I need to figure out what to tell him."

Milo rolled up Carl's sleeping bag and tucked it under an arm. "And isn't the film crew coming back this afternoon to show the shell of the building with the demo done? Are we going to try to keep this from them?"

14

Iris managed to get in another hour of sleep before heading to her 8:00 a.m. meeting with Alex Harcon at the Charles Hotel restaurant. She found Alex sitting at a corner table scrolling through his phone with a series of tiny, empty cups lined up in an arc in front of him.

Alex stood as she approached. "Hello there." He looked sheepishly down at the cups. "I figured I'd save time and order six espressos at once. I'm trying to get jump-started. What can I get you?"

Iris put in her own order for an extra-large cup of jet fuel coffee and tried to organize her thoughts. How should she tell him about Carl getting attacked last night? Better to wait until after the filming. No sense casting a pall over their first day of filming at the building site.

"I hope they're not planning any close-ups of me." It was 5:00 a.m. California time. Despite being immaculately dressed in one of his signature bespoke suits, Alex was looking every one of his forty-six years.

"You've been on TV before, right? The make-up person can work wonders. And *you* won't have to wear bright red lipstick."

Iris spotted Glen Forester's unmistakable thatch of bleached blond hair over by the restaurant entrance, stood up to catch his eye, and waved him over.

Glen's mood was annoyingly chipper for the hour. "Mr. Harcon, great to see you again." Glen pumped Alex's hand enthusiastically. "And Iris, are we all set for the groundbreaking?"

"We sure are." Iris tried to match Glen's animation. "Although you know we're not literally shoveling any dirt today."

His face fell. "We're not? Can't we fake it? Just a ceremonial dip with a shovel before we proceed to the script we discussed?"

"We're keeping the existing perimeter foundation of the building and the basement floor is concrete," she explained. "There's no dirt to shovel. Unless..."

Glen looked hopeful. "Unless?"

"There's a weed-infested piece of land out the back basement door." Iris said. "We can go out there wearing our hard hats and Alex can dig up some dirt for you."

Alex smiled. "You gotta love manufactured drama."

Glen made some notes on his phone. "Excellent. We'll meet Milo and his crew first, then Iris can give us a tour of the building with the work going on around her. After that, we'd like you, Alex, to tell us how you chose this building as your site. Did you consider other cities, other locations around Boston or Cambridge? Finally, you and Iris can show the audience the drawings laid out on the makeshift sawhorse table and discuss how the design evolved. Were there arguments about different approaches? Audiences love conflict. Play up any disagreements you might have had."

"About the order, Glen," Iris said. "I think we need to introduce Milo last. As soon as his crew is here, they'll want to start demolition on the partition walls upstairs. Once the pry bars start swinging, there'll be noise and plaster dust everywhere. I told Milo to come in at 10:00, so you could film Alex and me first. Does that work?"

"I see your point. Okay, I'll tell Nili to shift the sequence. Now we'd better head over there. Tonya needs you in makeup, Iris." Glen squinted at Alex. "And maybe some tinted concealer under the eyes for you."

The building site was a three-minute walk from the Charles Hotel. Iris had forgotten about these warm days of Indian Summer, and she began to perspire in her wool pantsuit. She took off the jacket and slung it over her shoulder.

A rusty twenty-yard dumpster and a video production van were parked in front of their building site in the curbside spaces Milo had reserved from the city. A building permit was posted in the front window, as required. Iris was surprised to see Milo already there, slouching against the building, waiting. Had he gone home at all this morning?

Iris introduced Milo to Glen and Alex, although Alex had already met Milo earlier when he'd conducted a thorough interview of the contractor.

"I texted you. You didn't need to come in until 10:00," Iris said. "We have to film some other segments first."

Milo gave her a sad half-smile. "My insurance policy says I need to make sure everyone on the site stays safe during construction or it's my ass. I'm here, and my guys are coming in at 10:00."

They found the film crew inside, busily setting up their equipment around a sawhorse table. Iris felt the rush she always felt at the start of demolition on a new project: the beginning of the Cinderella before-and-after transformation.

Nili looked up from a discussion with the photography director and walked over to join them. "You're really going to make this place look like that model we saw?"

Iris wished he didn't sound so incredulous in front of Alex. "That's the idea."

The dusty office building did look pretty shabby, with a worn vinyl tile floor and humming fluorescent lights suspended from a stained acoustical tile ceiling. But Iris could visualize it after its planned metamorphosis.

Tonya came hurrying over. She eyed Iris, Alex, and Milo, stopping when she got to Milo's black leather pants. "You the contractor? I like your style." She held up the plastic cape to Iris. "I need you in the chair first."

Fifteen minutes later, Iris's makeup had been dialed up several notches, and Tonya had managed to erase most of Alex's signs of fatigue. Iris, Milo, and Alex donned white Reid Associates hard hats and followed the crew down the stairs, and out to the backyard for the ground-breaking photo-op.

15

That morning, Jim Dugan couldn't get his nerve up to tell Trent he'd failed to recover the bones. He checked the *BostonGlobe.com* website on his phone before work. Any news of the break-in would show up online before hitting the print papers.

So far, so good. No mention of the crazy lumberjack who'd collided with his crowbar. The police might just take the guy for a homeless person who'd broken into an abandoned building, tripped, and fallen forward, hitting his head. Or maybe the guy rallied and staggered off under his own steam.

No one had ever figured out Jim's role in killing that kid twenty years ago. Why shouldn't his luck continue to hold?

At work, his morning was packed giving back-to-back golf lessons to overweight, middle-aged men with hopeless swings. The gloves rubbing against his scraped knuckles made the hours seem even more agonizing. It wasn't until noon that he got to take a break. He made his way to the golf club's restaurant and ordered his usual overstuffed steak sandwich with extra fries and a large Coke, overpriced if you actually had to pay for it. He needed the caffeine to keep him awake after barely four hours of sleep the night before. He sat at a corner table, away from the other diners, so that no one would notice his hands once he removed his golf gloves.

As Jim began his meal, he finally had a chance to check the *BostonGlobe.com* website on his phone for news. Three bites into his sandwich, he spotted an article: **Man Attacked in Harvard Square Building.** Jim coughed and almost spit out his last bite.

The article described a carpenter named Carl Nowak, who was sleeping in a building he was working on, when he was attacked in the middle of the night by an intruder wielding an iron bar. *Geez—this made it sound like he hit the guy on purpose. It was an accident!* Mr. Nowak was in critical condition at Mount Auburn Hospital. Jim felt a wave of relief. At least the guy hadn't died. He told himself that the doctors should be able to fix him up.

Then Jim saw a fuzzy photo of "the suspect": him, with his hoodie shielding the top half of his face. Damn those security cameras! Luckily, the photo was dark. Even his mother couldn't recognize him in that picture. The article ended with an appeal to call the 1-800 tip line if anyone had seen this suspect the previous night.

With a pounding heart, Jim sat back in his chair. He'd parked last night in a garage on the far side of the Square, then left an hour later. Would the police check on details like that and find it suspicious? Should he come up with an alibi, like a match.com date that had proved disastrous? But then he'd have to provide someone's name and where they'd arranged to meet. It wasn't as if he knew any woman who could be counted on to lie for him.

Jim nervously fingered the burner phone in his pocket. Maybe it was time to call Trent for help. Didn't he say they were in this together?

He wiped the sweat from his forehead. Who was he kidding? Trent was actually the greater threat. Especially now that the police were involved. Jim knew he'd now be nothing more than a convenient scapegoat.

16

Trent Westbrook stared without seeing out the back window of the destroyer-class Navigator as his driver negotiated the winding route to his campaign headquarters. He couldn't believe that someone else had a grip on his future, much less that lumbering fool, Jimbo Dugan. The guy hadn't even had the guts to call Trent on the burner phone, so surely, he'd failed in his assignment. After numerous unanswered calls to him, Trent had learned about the fiasco on a digital news site: **Man Attacked in Harvard Square Construction Site**. There was even a hazy security camera picture of Jimbo, luckily too dark and blurry to show much. The cops had sent out appeals for information from anyone who'd been in the neighborhood in the middle of the night and might have seen anything.

Trent pieced together what had happened. Okay, encountering a random carpenter sleeping in the building might not be anticipated. But had Trent been doing this himself, he would have taken the guy out with his unregistered Glock and followed through with the mission. Instead, it looked like Jimbo had panicked. You couldn't rely on anybody but yourself these days.

Would this construction crew need to lift those floorboards for the renovation? Maybe he'd get lucky, and the workers wouldn't touch the subfloor. That old sack of bones could be entombed under the new marble flooring forever. But Trent couldn't entrust his fate to luck. He needed a backup plan.

Shit. If the cops ever connected him to that dried-out skeleton, he stood to lose everything. Not only his political career. Not only Deidra and her family's money. He realized he could even go to jail.

For God's sake, the kid they had killed had been on the streets and was, no doubt, a junkie. His days were already numbered. And really, Kegs and Jimbo were the ones who had pushed the guy over the edge, not him. Trent's alibi, if it came to that, could be that he wasn't even there. He'd just heard about it at school afterward from his friends.

After all, one of these friends wasn't around to dispute the story, and the other would soon be confronting an unfortunate accident of his own.

17

After the morning's filming was over, Iris walked Alex back to the Charles Hotel. On the way, she said, "There's something I need to fill you in on. Let's go to the lounge." She informed him about the break-in.

Alex sat back in his chair, absorbing the news. Iris waited for a reaction.

Finally, he asked, "Is the carpenter going to be all right?"

"I just checked with Milo who's in touch with Carl's wife. They're waiting to see how much damage was caused by his fractured skull and the bleeding in his brain. It could take days for them to tell. Carl may have to go to rehab to relearn certain functions, like walking and talking."

Alex sighed heavily. "That's terrible. I'll want to speak with the doctors and make certain he's getting the best care possible. I assume that Mr. Nowak's camping out in the building wasn't sanctioned by Milo."

"No. Carl is Milo's head carpenter, and he had a key on him after they'd moved in their tools yesterday. If Milo ever gets delayed, he wants to be sure someone else can let the crew in to start working."

"Will Milo be short-handed while Mr. Nowak recuperates? Not that the schedule isn't flexible."

"I haven't discussed that with him yet. I know he has back-up people he can bring in."

"And the building itself was not damaged?"

"Milo and I inspected it ourselves. We saw nothing missing or vandalized. Not that there was much there to steal at this stage of work."

"Such strange timing. What have the police said about a possible motive?"

"While the crew and Milo were being filmed, I called the police station and spoke with a Lieutenant Garcia, who's in charge of the case. He didn't share much information, just asked me questions. He sent out a city-wide flyer this morning to all the neighborhood listserves asking if anyone saw the suspect last night, around 2:00 a.m." Iris pulled a copy of the flyer out of her purse and slid it across the table. "This is a blurry shot from a security camera near an ATM at that time of a possible suspect carrying a big duffle bag. This might or might not be him, given that Harvard Square attracts a lot of late-night action and odd characters."

Alex studied the photo under the 'Have you seen this man?' heading. "Dark hoodie pulled low. You can't see his features."

"I know."

Alex tilted his head to one side. "If this is the guy, I wonder what he was hoping to steal that would fit inside that duffle bag?"

18

Iris arrived back at the building site at 3:30, fifteen minutes before Nili asked her to be there to prep for more filming. He wanted to show how the first day of demolition work had progressed. The front door was propped open.

She spotted Milo in the atrium on his knees tearing up squares of vinyl with a pry bar. Two other workers were busy with the same task.

"Hey, Milo," she called out. "Any updates on Carl?"

"Not yet." He reached into his back pocket and handed her two shiny new keys. "For the front and basement doors."

Iris tucked the key inside her purse.

"How's the work coming along?"

He stood up, looked around, and stretched his back. "Slowly. I'm not sure how photogenic the place is going to look in half an hour."

"Just sweep up the dust. It's supposed to look like a construction site. It will make the final reveal be that much more impressive."

Milo gave the younger of the two demo workers a push broom and instructions. "Did you get any information out of the police?"

Iris showed him the flyer. "Lieutenant Garcia is in charge, and he thinks this ATM photo might be of the intruder. He sent out a bulletin asking if anyone saw him last night."

A harsh laugh escaped Milo's throat, and he handed the paper back to her. "This shot could be of my grandmother. A lot of good that's going to do. Did Garcia say they got the crowbar, or whatever Carl was hit with?"

"Wouldn't tell me. An ongoing investigation. Yadda, yadda... By the way, Harcon doesn't think we should mention the break-in and Carl's injury to the film crew."

Milo gave her a level look. "Of course he doesn't." He went back to work while Iris wandered around the first and second floors, marveling at how different the space looked with walls removed.

At 4:00, she heard the film crew enter and picked her way down the stairs to meet them.

Milo was still tearing up tiles under the staircase. He turned to Nili. "You want us to stop working?"

Nili looked around the space. "No, this would make a good shot, with most of the walls down and you and the other guys demonstrating how demo gets done. We'll set up our equipment. Iris, let Tonya get some make-up on you. Your jeans look fine since this is a construction day, but please put on a blazer or something more finished. Where's Harcon?"

Iris checked her watch. "He should be here any minute."

While the crew busied themselves, James set up his camera, focusing on Milo, who was muttering under his breath and trying to ignore the attention.

Iris sat on a folding chair in the section of the atrium where the flooring had already been stripped as Tonya accentuated Iris's eyes and mouth, then puffed a generous coat of powder on her face. Iris tried not to sneeze and mentally ran through the dialogue she'd prepared for this segment.

Alex arrived and apologized to Nili for being late. "I got tied up with phone calls." Iris noticed that the two top buttons of his dress shirt were unfastened, and his sleeves were rolled to his elbows as a concession to demolition day. Tonya steered toward him with her powder puff.

Nili clapped his hands to call for everyone's attention. "Good afternoon, people. We'll start with a view of the atrium showing the newly opened space and the workers finishing up the floor demo. Milo can give us a few words telling us about the demolition process. Then, Iris, you'll enter from that side and walk us through the building, pointing out the walls and other elements that have been removed. James will follow you with the hand-held camera. We'll wrap up back here in the atrium with Iris describing the next framing phase to Mr. Harcon, with the skeletons of the new curving staircase and cantilevered balconies getting built." Nili checked that everyone was in their places, then said, "Action."

Iris watched as James slowly panned his camera around the space, then closed in on Milo's rear end in his black leather pants, framed by his tool belt. Milo turned and gave him an irritated look.

Nili made a rolling gesture with his hand for Milo to start talking.

Milo faced the camera. "We're finishing the second day of demolition and all the partition walls which the architect wanted removed have been taken down and carted away to the dumpster. Ms. Reid already made sure that none of these were structurally bearing. We've had to be careful to leave electrical wiring and plumbing pipes intact for the time being. This staircase—" Milo gestured to his left. "—needs to remain until we can frame a new one. At the moment, we're removing certain surfaces, like this vinyl flooring, so we can inspect the framing underneath to verify its strength to hold up the new marble floor without cracking."

Nili gave Milo a thumbs up and Iris walked into the shot to start her tour of the other first-floor rooms. She tried to remember not to swing her arms around for emphasis as much as she'd done the day before. The small entourage circled back and headed up the stairs.

Iris finished her excursion through the upper floors and returned to the ground level with James following behind, supporting the camera on his shoulder.

Milo was industriously prying up a subfloor board under the staircase. Iris and James moved closer to give the viewers a look at the floor joists. Iris was prepared with a tape measure in her hand to discuss whether the joists were deep enough to hold up the new marble. Alex joined them for this faux drama since their structural engineer had analyzed the existing framing design long before and decided what additional reinforcement would be needed.

Iris noticed a small edge of plastic sheeting visible as Milo pried back the board. A vapor barrier? She moved closer.

Milo gave the four-foot-long board a final tug, and it swung up, exposing what appeared to be a plastic-wrapped package. The grip shined a light on it. Four heads and a camera leaned in to examine it closer, then recoiled.

The bleached white dome of a cranium, with the twin hollows of eye sockets and a crooked picket fence of teeth stared back at them.

19

Milo dropped the heavy plank, nearly hitting his foot. "Holy shit!" He turned to Iris. "You see that?"

The blood rushed in her ears. "Yeah, and it looks real." She noticed James was still filming, so she turned away from the cameraman and caught Alex's eye. She tipped her head toward a far corner, and he followed her away from the group. Milo trailed behind, brushing off his hands on his pants.

They huddled together. Alex spoke in a low voice, indecipherable to anyone more than a whisper away. "I agree. It looks real, and it looks old. We need to call someone." He turned to Milo. "Did that vinyl and the subfloor look like they'd been lifted recently?"

Milo's eyes widened. "Like last-night-recently when the intruder was here? You think he might have planted it?" Milo considered for a moment. "Nah. That flooring was intact. No cuts in the vinyl. No one messed with it since it was originally installed, probably before I was born."

Alex frowned. "Assuming this skeleton is real, it certainly didn't bury itself under those floorboards. Iris, can you call that police officer in charge of the break-in? He can figure out whose jurisdiction this falls under."

Iris slid her phone out of her pocket and keyed in Lieutenant Joe Garcia's number she'd plugged into her contacts. Garcia told her to keep everyone away from the discovery area and for them to refrain from telling anyone about this or posting anything on social media. He said he would be there shortly with a forensics team.

Iris hurried over to the film crew, who were circled around Tonya's impromptu make-up area. Several of them were clutching their phones. "Please put down your phones. The police will be here soon. They don't want any news about these remains leaking before they can properly investigate."

Alex walked over to Nili. "If this turns out to be a crime site, I don't want that included in the film. The body would have been hidden under the stairs long before I bought the building, and it's not part of the image I want to create for the museum."

Nili half-smiled. "There's also the theory that all publicity is good publicity. People might want to watch the film and come to the museum *just because* a body was found here."

"Maybe Glen and I should discuss this." Alex walked away.

Ten minutes after Iris had phoned him, Lieutenant Garcia arrived, accompanied by a small team. The detective looked to be about Iris's age and had a failed goatee of straggling hairs. A younger companion detective in a coat and tie stood behind him, along with several crime scene technicians in Tyvek jumpsuits and booties.

Iris made a few introductions. Alex stepped in and took over the interaction with the police. He explained the events leading up to the discovery and led the group over to the staircase. Iris forced herself to smile but was gritting her teeth at being elbowed aside.

Garcia asked Alex to dismiss the film crew and Milo's carpenters. Alex, Iris, and Milo were allowed to remain, in case Garcia had questions for them.

Milo held up his pry bar. "Do you want me to, um, lift off more boards?"

Garcia shook his head. "Thanks, we'll take it from here. This is a crime scene, however old, and we can't have anything in this area disturbed. You three should stand back, if you please."

Garcia and the other detective put on their own white jumpsuits and booties and stood near the staircase. Lights flashed as a tech took photos, while another slowly pried open the subfloor to expose the full plastic-wrapped skeleton. Iris leaned forward to see longer bones below the skull—the ribcage, arms, and legs. The parcel had been squeezed in between the joists, which were spaced only sixteen inches apart. So, the body, before it decomposed, must have been small, or at least pretty thin. Was it a child? More pictures were taken, then the forensic team lifted the wrapped package of bones out of its niche and laid it on the adjacent floor.

Garcia asked Milo the same question that Alex had. "Did the floor look like the surface had been cut into?"

Milo stuffed his hands in his pockets. "I didn't notice any seams."

Garcia turned to Iris and Alex. "Do you know when this place was built?"

Iris answered, "1974, according to the building department records."

The four of them heard the front door slam shut and looked over. A petite woman with cat-eye glasses entered the atrium. Garcia introduced her as Dr. Lisa Graham, the medical examiner. She moved over to join the forensic techs.

They carefully unwrapped the thick plastic shroud. A slightly putrefied odor emerged. Brownish splotches had stained some of the bones. Bits of clothing clung to other sections. Iris could see clumps of black hair still attached to the sides of the skull.

Dr. Graham knelt beside the skeleton. Her eyes darted to Garcia's. "Definitely human. The victim's been dead for several decades. I'll do the testing back in my office, but I doubt it's been here since 1974. I can analyze the material. That might give us the timeframe."

Garcia crossed his arms. "This one belongs to cold cases."

Dr. Graham nodded. "Definitely." She looked closely at some small bones near the center of the skeleton. "Now this is interesting."

Garcia leaned in for a closer look."

The medical examiner continued, "It looks like the bones in the hands have been smashed."

20

After the medical examiner's team had transported the human remains to their van, Alex suggested that Iris and Milo join him at the Harvest restaurant for a drink to steady their nerves. It was 5:00 p.m. and the Harvard Square work crowd was disgorging from low-rise office buildings crowding the brick sidewalks. Many were entering or exiting the Red Line subway station, fighting their way home.

The trio walked two blocks and turned down an alley, entering the restaurant through its inconspicuous door. Alex spoke quietly to the maître-d' and they were ushered to a corner booth in the softly lit bar area with no other patrons nearby. Incongruous in a place as elegant as this, two TVs were switched on over the bar, one set to a Red Sox game, the other to CNN. Fortunately, the sound was set low.

Iris and Milo slid into a banquette facing Alex. Iris studied the wine and cocktail list, wondering if she should stick to something non-alcoholic. What the hell. It wasn't as if she and Alex hadn't shared a good number of drinks before. However, she still felt a little resentful that Alex had taken the lead with the police, and she didn't want her feelings to show. Iris went ahead and ordered a Trimbach Riesling, promising herself she would stick to a single glass.

Alex didn't even glance at the menu before ordering a glass of Nebbiolo. "And perhaps a cheese plate with some crackers?" He smiled charmingly at the female server, who seemed all too aware of who he was.

Her rock musician/contractor, on the other hand, looked totally unintimidated to find himself drinking with one of the wealthiest men in the country. "Blanton Bourbon-rocks," Milo tossed out nonchalantly.

When the server had left, Alex said, "Hell of a day. I'm beginning to wonder, Iris, if all your projects feature corpses."

"Only when my clients buy sites with the bodies pre-stashed." *Oops. Did that sound snarky?* She smiled. Milo gave her a kick under the table.

"We'll need to set up better security measures." Alex looked at Milo. "I'll have my team from California get in touch with you tomorrow. We can use a system like the one we used on the Medford Art Studios."

Milo nodded.

Alex's attention wandered to his phone. "I'm scheduled to fly back to California in the morning. Do you think everything is under control now?"

Milo answered, "Garcia said the construction can proceed because he wouldn't designate the property as a crime scene. The police will follow up on the cold case under the stairs, but any evidence from twenty years ago would be long gone."

"My thought exactly," Alex said. "The police can figure out that old mystery without affecting our project. And as far as the film goes, I'll have Glen cut out that segment when Milo lifts the floorboard. We should be fine."

Their drinks arrived. Alex cut up some cheese and passed the plate around. Iris had been hungry until the image of the slender skeleton with smashed hands popped into her mind. She wished she could highlight and delete the image. "Why did someone break its hands?" *Wait. Did I say that out loud?*

Milo stopped in mid-sip and put his glass down. "Those bones might have gotten broken when the body was stuffed into the floor."

They both knew how implausible that was, but Iris appreciated Milo's effort to soften her memory.

She felt a sudden desire to get home and spend the evening with her dog. After chit-chatting for another half hour about the filming and the construction phase ahead, Iris finished her drink and made her excuses to leave. She risked a look at Milo. He met her eyes and, with a raised eyebrow, wordlessly asked if she was all right. She gave him a brief nod and left.

21

As soon as Iris got home, she removed the camera make-up and changed into her baggy sleep T-shirt and fuzzy socks. Luc was busy downstairs cooking for the Wednesday night dinner crowd. This was the problem with being in love with a successful chef. He was so often working just when she wanted to unwind together at the end of the day or go out on the town. So, instead, she shared the news of her traumatic day with her trusty Basset hound. After scavenging in the fridge for some leftover chicken for Sheba, she fixed herself a ham and cheese sandwich.

The dog seemed to listen, glancing up several times from her bowl to cast sympathetic looks toward Iris. They both moved to the living room and Iris settled down on the sofa. Sheba circled three times, then curled into a ball at her feet.

"No mooching my dinner." Iris slid her sandwich farther away from the ever-hopeful dog and reached for the TV remote. She turned on the Boston 7 o'clock news. The lead story featured a live shot of the outside of Iris's building site with a chyron unwinding: ***Human Remains Found Under Staircase in Harvard Square Building.***

"Oh, shit!" Her dog looked at her with alarm. "Sorry, Sheba. Bad language."

How had the story leaked to the press jackals already? She supposed it was impossible to hide anything of interest that happened in the middle of a dense, talkative city, especially with a dozen people on site when the remains had been found.

Iris listened to the excited newscaster in her bright red blouse and vivid lipstick talking about the discovery. "This is the building in Harvard Square that financier and inventor Alex Harcon is turning into a museum to showcase his personal art collection. During the demolition today, carpenters uncovered a set of human remains under the floorboards. The medical examiner has made a preliminary determination that the remains are of a male in his late teens who would have died around twenty years ago. Police are looking into unsolved missing person cases from that era. Anyone with information pertaining to this death is urged to call the police help line at the bottom of the screen."

At least it wasn't the skeleton of a child. And they hadn't mentioned her name, or Milo's. Yet. When the broadcast moved on to the next sensational story, Iris turned off the TV.

So, it was a teenager, and he must have had a slight build to fit between the joists. If he was a murder victim, had he been killed in the building or moved there afterward? Iris couldn't stop thinking about his delicate, smashed hands. The newscaster hadn't mentioned them. She couldn't imagine how much that mutilation would hurt. As an architect, losing the ability of her hands to draw would be a nightmare. Had someone been sending a message? About stealing? Did this scrawny guy steal drugs from some dealer and get killed in return? God knew, Harvard Square could be a mecca for drug deals, especially in that era.

Iris chewed her sandwich absently. Alex's main concern had been about possible delay for his project, adding security to the building, and avoiding negative press coverage of his new museum. He didn't seem to be affected by the long-ago death at all. She hadn't noticed that apparent callousness the previous summer when they'd been searching for the high-tech weapon that had been stolen from him. But that crime would have felt more personal. Iris guessed you didn't rise to the top of the business world with your empathy chip fully enabled.

But Milo had felt some sadness for the long-deceased victim. She had seen it in his eyes. Interesting man, her contractor. And he had faced another much more personal tragedy today. His lead carpenter had been attacked at the job site and lay in the hospital with potential brain damage. Was that just this morning? Iris remembered seeing Carl's sleeping bag in the alcove under the staircase.

The thought stopped her. She stared at Sheba. "No way!"

Were these events connected? Had the intruder been intending to uncover the human remains when he encountered Carl? Had he been planning to stash the bones in that duffle bag he was carrying?

22

Trent changed into a French cuffed shirt and navy pin-striped suit in the suite his campaign had rented at the Copley Plaza. Once Deirdra arrived, they would descend the grand staircase to the main ballroom and meet with Trent's biggest donors, including Deirdra's wealthy parents.

He affixed his American flag cufflinks and completed the Windsor knot in his tie. As he adjusted his breast pocket square, a glance in the mirror revealed Edward Weber standing in the doorway. "Thanks for coming. Come in and close the door," Trent said, keeping his voice low. "I need your expertise on a delicate matter."

Edward was a former Army Ranger, platinum-haired with coldly watchful eyes. Trent had met Edward back when he was still a lowly State Rep, starting his climb up the political ladder. Soon enough, Trent became a national congressman, and put Edward on his staff as head of security. The man's efficient dispatch of Kegs had proven his skill and discretion. During Trent's recent run for the U.S. Senate, Edward had been invaluable in smoothing the path in any number of ways, legal and otherwise.

"Remember that unfortunate sailing accident of my friend in Gloucester?"

"Yes, sir. Back in March of 2019, I believe. Tragic."

"Another friend from high school, James Dugan, a golf pro at the Country Club in Brookline, may be about to have his own accident. Possibly, a vehicular one."

"Rotten luck. You have my condolences in advance, sir."

"Let me know when it's taken care of, please, and thank you, Edward."

"Of course. Anything else?"

"I'm assuming you have the security detail in place in the ballroom?"

"Yes, sir."

"Good, good."

As Edward opened the door to leave, Trent spotted Tina Chung, his Chief of Staff, hand in the air, about to knock. She moved aside to let the head of security pass.

"Ah, come on in, Tina. How's it looking out there?"

"The room is filling up." She checked the time on her phone. "Do you want me to call Deirdra? Make sure her driver isn't stuck on the Pike?"

"Let's give her a few more minutes. She's usually so punctual." Trent handed Tina a few marked-up sheets of paper. "I made a few changes to tonight's speech. Can you have the teleprompter updated, please?"

"Sure thing. I'll take these down now."

Tina left just as Deirdra passed her and swished into the room in a coral tea-length gown. Her blond hair was perfectly coifed, although a bit big for New England, and she wore serious jewelry. "Sorry, dear. There was a long line getting into the hotel garage. But that's a sure sign that your event will be well-attended. Which speech are you giving tonight? Hopefully, not the one about helping the poor homeless people again."

"But dearest, that's my signature cause. I want all the reporters to mention it in the papers and websites tomorrow morning."

"It's just that, you know, the subject makes Mother and Daddy uncomfortable."

23

Early on Tuesday morning, Iris headed over to the museum site. Milo's crew was scheduled to start framing that day, which didn't require her supervision since all the architectural requirements were carefully laid out in the drawing set. But she felt a strong need to be there.

She stopped at Simon's Coffee on Mass Ave to get Milo a cup of the organic, non-caffeinated tea that he liked.

When she entered the building, she spotted him in a small room off the entryway, turned away from her. His head was resting against the wall and his hand, clasping his phone, hung at his side.

She knocked on the open doorframe. "Milo?"

When he turned around, his eyes were red, and his expression desolate.

"What happened?"

"Gail called." Milo's voice was barely audible. "A blood vessel in Carl's brain burst overnight. The doctors aren't sure he'll survive much longer, but if he does, he'll have major long-term problems. Like a stroke, I guess, times ten."

Iris bit down on her bottom lip. She set the cup of tea on the floor and walked over to give Milo a hug. They stood there for a moment, arms wrapped around each other. She pulled back. "I'm so sorry."

Milo's Adam's apple moved up and down in a silent, anguished gulp. "I've known Carl for four years. We started out as carpenters, both working for K+R Construction. He was the one who urged me to get my contractor's license."

She felt an ache in her chest and wanted to comfort him. She handed him the cup of tea, which was no doubt cold by now. "He sounds like a good friend."

He stared at the cup in his hand. "Yeah, thanks. I don't understand why he didn't come to my place instead of coming here." His phone buzzed, and he glanced at it. "It's Garcia."

He answered, "Miller." He listened for a few moments. "Okay. I'm at the building."

"What did he want?"

"He says there may be a tie-in between Carl's assault and the skeleton. The intruder might have been trying to dig up the bones."

"That's exactly what I was thinking!" Her pulse accelerated. "I was just about to tell you. The guy came with a crowbar and a duffle bag. The victim, with those smashed hands, was most likely murdered and whoever did it might be afraid the construction work would expose the remains, or any evidence left behind."

Milo looked skeptical. "After twenty years? It's hard to believe there'd be anything incriminating still here."

"Haven't you ever seen those CSI shows? The forensic techs and the medical examiner use dental records or DNA or even fragments of clothing to track down the victim's identity. Then the police try to locate their associates or enemies to find the murderer."

Milo closed his eyes. "I just want whoever attacked Carl to get locked away forever in a tiny goddamn cell."

"I know."

They heard loud knocking on the front door and went to open it. Lieutenant Garcia was standing there by himself. He looked over at

Iris. "Good. Ms. Reid. I'm glad to see you're here, as well. Mr. Harcon told us he was headed back to California this morning."

Milo folded his arms across his chest. "I don't know if you've been informed, but a blood vessel burst in Carl Nowak's head last night. He's barely hanging on. Have you found the bastard who did this yet?"

"That's why I'm here, Mr. Miller. We're taking his case very seriously. We're working with the hypothesis that Mr. Nowak's assailant was here trying to retrieve the remains you found yesterday under the floorboards."

"Has the Medical Examiner identified those remains?" Iris asked.

"Tying the cold case in with the recent assault on Mr. Nowak moves its priority up, so we hope to be getting results soon."

"Were the hands smashed pre- or postmortem?" Iris asked.

Garcia regarded her with a guarded look. "I can't go into that with you at this point. It's an ongoing investigation."

"Okay," Iris said. "How about this then? Did you collect samples of the blood that was on the floor after Carl was attacked?"

"What blood are you referring to?"

Milo pointed. "There were signs of a scuffle in the dust on the floor. Iris and I saw drops of blood there. It could have been Carl's, or it could have been his attacker's. Do you mean to tell me your guys didn't even notice it?"

Garcia walked over to where Milo had pointed. "Oh, yeah. We took a sample of some drops of blood. But so much dust got mixed in with it during the scuffle that it was contaminated. There was no useable evidence."

24

A few minutes later, a team of forensic technicians arrived, and went through the process of suiting up. Iris wondered what evidence they hoped to find after the construction and film crews had trampled and thoroughly disturbed the site. Garcia led them over to the area under the staircase and spoke to them in a low voice. The subfloor boards were still stacked in a pile, leaving the skeleton's hiding place open to view.

Iris and Milo watched the search from the far side of the atrium. Camera flashes burst as a photographer documented every surface between the joists, looking for marks or traces of evidence. Some techs branched out slowly in a grid pattern, studying the surrounding floors and walls. Evidently tying the cold case in with a recent investigation allowed for a more substantial effort to be spent searching for clues.

Milo slammed the flat of his hand against a wall and glared at Garcia. "Did you really conduct a proper investigation yesterday when some lowly carpenter got whacked over the head with a crowbar? Or have you come back now because those bagged up remains turned out to be someone important? Is that why you're all of a sudden paying attention?"

Garcia walked over to Milo and returned the glare. "No one gets favored status here. Your lowly carpenter's injuries are now life-threatening. That's what's changed the nature of this investigation."

Iris pulled him aside. "Milo, this has got to be a nightmare for you. Would you like me to stay to keep an eye on this so you can check on Carl at the hospital?"

Milo ran his hands through his hair. "Carl might die. The guy who attacked him should be locked up by now. But that would require the cops to give a shit and do their jobs."

Iris held his gaze. "Antagonizing them is not going to help. Why don't you go down to the hospital and find out how Carl's doing?"

Milo gave his head a shake, turned, and strode out of the building.

Iris moved over, closer to the staircase.

"Lieutenant!" the photographer called out. "I think we found something."

Iris rushed over behind Garcia and saw what the photographer was pointing to. A tiny piece of blue material, just bigger than a nail head, was caught on a screw poking through one of the exposed timber joists.

"Good work. Document it and bag it. We'll need to make sure it wasn't torn off yesterday when the carpenters pulled up the boards."

Iris spoke up. "If it helps, I don't think so. Milo was the only one near those joists yesterday before the police arrived and he was dressed all in black, like he always is." She asked Lieutenant Garcia if she could see the evidence bag with the scrap of blue fabric up close.

He held it out for her. "You recognize this?"

Iris peered at the piece of material. "It's too small to tell what this came from, but that color is distinctive—I think it's between an Aegean blue and a Mediterranean blue on the Pantone color chart."

"If you say so." Garcia rolled his eyes, took back the bag, and handed it to a forensic tech. "Send this to Hair and Fibers for analysis."

Where had she seen that shade of blue before? Could identifying this scrap lead to finding out who that sad bag of remains had once been? Or who had murdered him? This was going to drive her crazy. But she hoped the CSI specialists could figure it out.

Iris climbed the stairs to the second floor to check in with Dewey, Milo's new second-in-command. The buzzing and thumping of the air compressors, nail guns, and occasional hammering told her that the framing was proceeding at a good pace. Three carpenters were nailing together wood studs for the new walls. She approached a huge man with a red ponytail and a Celtic knot tattoo running across his neck.

Iris had to shout to be heard. "How's it going?"

Dewey glanced at her, walked over to the air compressor, and switched it off. The room got altogether quiet. "We're moving along. Is Milo coming up to help?"

"He went to the hospital to check on Carl."

Three other sizable carpenters watched her now, thumbs looped in their tool belts, gazing downward. Dewey broke the brief silence. "He's gonna be okay, isn't he?"

So, it seemed that Milo hadn't told the crew about Carl's burst blood vessel. "I don't know. Maybe Milo can give you an update when he gets back. I'm really sorry about Carl."

Dewey nodded. "Thanks."

The concern and pain in the air were palpable. These men were close. Iris felt like an intruder. "Call me if you have any questions. I'll be back tomorrow when you're laying out the new staircase."

She descended to the first floor. The CSI technicians and Garcia had finished up and left. When Iris reached the sidewalk, she noticed a supermarket bouquet, wrapped in cellophane, set near the door as a memorial. She wondered if the person who left it might have known the dead man's identity or if it was a general, sympathetic reflex to a tragedy. She looked around to see if she could find the donor and ask, but as she scanned the swirl of pedestrian traffic, there were no obvious candidates.

25

Trent was on a tight schedule today. Between visits to a running shoe factory up in Lowell, a diner out in Fitchburg for another heartburn-inducing lunch with the mayor, and an elementary school in Lynn, he had a full day ahead. But he lingered over his morning coffee, making sure he'd caught all the media coverage of his fundraiser the previous night.

"Don't you need to get going, dear?" Deirdra looked up at him from across the breakfast table.

"The *Boston Herald* only gave my speech three lines on the Local News page," Trent complained.

"It doesn't matter," Deirdra fed a bite of toast to the elderly Bichon Frisé on her lap. "You know their readers aren't our people."

"Yeah, true." Trent's attention was caught by the headline directly above his three lines. **Human Remains Found Under Staircase in Harvard Square Building.** He scanned the text and let out a "Shit!" before he could compose himself.

"What's wrong?" Deirdra inquired.

"Uh, I just remembered, I need to meet Tina at HQ to put together a talk for the schoolkids in Lynn before we go up there." He swept all the newspapers into his briefcase to scrutinize later in the car and got up to give Deirdra a peck on the cheek. "See you tonight, dear."

Once he was ensconced in the womblike back seat of the Navigator, Trent read the *Herald* article more carefully. It figured that yesterday would turn out to be the day that the floor demo work would start up on that damn building. Could Jimbo have cut it any closer in planning his retrieval operation? And there was even a film crew there when the carpenters lifted the floorboards and discovered the remains of that kid! A certain amount of mission creep was unavoidable, but this was getting out of hand.

Trent noticed the alarmed look of his driver eyeing him in the rear-view mirror. He must have sworn out loud. He flipped through the other papers but found only one other mention of the incident in the *Globe*, reporting essentially the same information.

So, what were the implications for him? Had the police figured out that the break-in the night before was connected to the discovery beneath the floorboards? And even if they did suspect a link, was there any way they could tie him to either one? Unless, of course, Jimbo gave up the goods.

Trent closed the partition to the front seat and speed-dialed a number on this week's special burner phone. "I just read the paper, and—"

Edward interrupted, "I saw it, sir, and I understand. This makes it critical to find your friend. But you're not going to like this."

"Go on."

"James Dugan has done a runner. The golf club says he's on a leave of absence. They wouldn't give me any more details. I went by his condo, and it looked like some clothes were missing. I checked his credit cards and bank statements. He withdrew $5k, his limit, out of an ATM yesterday afternoon and took off in his car. Hasn't used his credit cards. I have the plate number of the car but haven't located it yet."

"Sounds like old Jimbo isn't as dumb as I thought. But wait. He has a son, doesn't he?"

"Yes, sir. Jimmy Junior. Seven years old. The kid lives with the ex-wife in Newton."

"So, we have some leverage. Give me time to think about this but keep trying to find Dugan."

26

Jim Dugan was not the type of guy to go on the lam. But after a sympathetic reception nurse at the Mount Auburn Hospital told him over the phone that Carl Nowak had suffered a brain hemorrhage, and he'd seen online that the construction crew had uncovered the kid's bones, his anxiety quotient hit the stratosphere. It was a matter of time before Trent or the police came for him. He wasn't sure whom he feared more.

Jim pulled his Subaru into a space on the top level of the Logan Airport Central Parking garage. Let his pursuers spin their wheels, checking out the various flights he might have taken. He hadn't watched all those cop shows on TV for nothing. He wheeled his suitcase over to the elevator, moved across a bridge into Terminal C, descended to the ground level, and strolled out to the bus stop. While he waited for the next Silver Line bus, he checked the schedule on his phone for Amtrak trains leaving South Station in the next hour.

There was nothing Jim could do to disguise his height and bulk, but he'd tried to dress like a typical tourist in a Red Sox sweatshirt, chinos, and a cap. He slipped on a pair of sunglasses as the bus approached South Station, a bustling transportation hub where the subway, buses, trains, and taxis intersected. Jim kept his head down as he hurried over to the counter to buy a train ticket with cash, conscious of the many security cameras that would be mounted in places like this.

Half an hour later, he was on his way to Washington, D.C. He figured he'd make his way west to some place where he could hide out cheaply, without attracting attention. Maybe Memphis or Little Rock. It wasn't as if he could cross over to Mexico or Canada without having his passport flagged.

As the Acela train gained speed through the Boston suburbs, he had time to reflect on this sorry state of affairs. Maybe this was karma. Over the last twenty years, he had never been able to forget the terrified look in the kid's eyes. Would the police be able to find any kind of forensic evidence to tie him to that awful murder? On TV shows, they always discover a tell-tale clue. And now, how about something tying him to Carl Nowak's death, which he still thoroughly believed was an accident? Had he left anything behind? He'd taken the crowbar and duffle bag away with him. Nowak hadn't gotten any of Jim's skin under his fingernails. It would be down to someone recognizing him on his trip to or from the garage. Or Trent ratting on him in some anonymous tip. But a tip couldn't be traced, right?

What would Jimmy Junior think about his father disappearing? He had written a letter to his ex-wife saying that he wouldn't be able to take the boy for a while since he had a personal emergency which he needed to deal with. He asked her to assure their son that he loved him and would be back to see him as soon as he could. Snail mail seemed like the best way to send it, since he was paranoid about the hackability of any electronic networks.

The Country Club had been okay about letting him take some personal time off on short notice. It was mid-October, so they were heading into the slow season, anyway. Would this whole business blow over in a few months so Jim could come home and resume his life?

27

As soon as Iris entered her office, Loretta flagged her down. "Boss, your project has gone viral." She frowned, "but maybe not in a good way."

Iris groaned and moved behind the reception desk so she could see Loretta's computer screen.

Loretta explained she had set a Google alert for any mention of the firm and her email had been flooded that afternoon. Loretta navigated to Twitter on her browser, and Iris saw endless rows of tweets. "It's mainly about the skeleton," Loretta said. "But a lot of tweets mention you or Alex Harcon. I'll send you a link so you can look at them in your office."

"Okay, I guess." Iris would have preferred to ignore the tweets, but she had to be prepared in case Alex brought them up.

Iris stopped by Rollo's desk on the way to her office. "How are the Brewster Street schematics coming along?"

"Almost done," Rollo said, "but I have an idea I want to run by you. You know where you've put a powder room under the new staircase? How about moving the door to the side like this?" He showed her on the drawing. "It would feel more private."

"That's a great idea. And why don't you join us at the meeting with the clients tomorrow? It's here in the conference room at 10:00."

"Sure." He looked surprised, but in a good way. Iris wanted to give Rollo plenty of responsibility to build his confidence and keep him happy as an employee. No question that it was hard to find good staff.

When Iris sat down at her desk, opened her laptop, and followed the link from Loretta, she landed on a thread called **Skeleton hidden under Harvard Square floor of Alex Harcons new museum. Haunted much? LOL.**

Damn. It had a close-up photo of the skull peeking through the plastic. Who had taken this picture and leaked it? One of the CSI techs? Or, more likely, someone from the film crew. Damn, again. She hoped that person would find themselves in deep trouble. Alex was going to flip out. The tweet was submitted by **@CrazyMazie79-3h,** which Iris supposed meant it was posted three hours ago. Great. There were already over 1,500 enthusiastic likes in response and many retweets.

Most were short. Things like: **cool, bet he paid extra for that, probably pr stunt, love the teeth…**

But one asked: **isn't this the iris reed project** Another said: **iris read will do anything for publicity** That one was signed **@OpheliaHamlet-1h**

How did these people get away with hiding behind fake names, and why couldn't they use punctuation or spell her name correctly? They could spew any trash they wanted without repercussions. Iris forced herself to skim quickly through the rest of the thread. Two hours ago, **@valerianmodi** tweeted: **show some respect remains might have been someones son/brother.** Directly after that **@pisces** tweeted: **my friend sam a good guy.**

Iris's skin prickled. Did **@pisces** know who their dead body was? Maybe even know the circumstances of how he got there?

She grabbed her cell phone and punched in Lieutenant Garcia's number.

28

Iris was surprised to learn that Lieutenant Garcia had already red-flagged the tweet from *@pisces*. Evidently, the Cambridge police were thoroughly up to speed on monitoring social media for any mentions that might be pertinent to their cases.

"Can you find out who *@pisces* is?" she asked him.

"First of all, we don't know if this person posting is really talking about our cold case. It could easily be some nutcase looking for attention."

"Or someone who knew the guy from twenty years ago who disappeared into that building and never came out."

"Ms. Reid, I've heard about your past help to the CPD, so I'm affording you some leeway with information I wouldn't normally give out. Please keep it confidential. We've already subpoenaed Twitter to get this message's IP address. We should be able to use that information to track down the service provider and subpoena them to disclose the account holder's name and maybe even get a physical address."

Iris took a sip from her metal water bottle. "How long does that take?"

"Depends on how responsive the service provider is. But if the person tweeting wanted to hide their identity, they only had to log on to this account from a public Wi-Fi access point, like Starbucks, or a library."

"*@pisces* didn't sound sophisticated or paranoid."

"Oh, you'd be amazed. Every other person on Twitter seems to be either a conspiracy-theorist or a catfisher."

After Garcia promised to tell her if he got any news, Iris ended the call and decided to check in with Milo. She texted:

> How's Carl doing?

He texted back:

> Not good. Docs aren't sure he'll survive the night. Hemorrhage was too big.

Iris was about to hit the "voice call" button to talk to him, then hesitated. Was this interfering too much? She wanted to reassure Milo that Carl would pull through, but that seemed wildly optimistic. So, she simply texted:

> I'm sorry to hear that. Let me know if I can do anything.

> Find the guy who did this to Carl so I can...

Milo stopped his text there and Iris could imagine him overcome with anger and grief.

How was she supposed to identify the shadowy figure in the security camera footage? The only clue they had about him was that he might have been there trying to retrieve the bones from under the staircase. And the one link they had to that old crime was the curious tweet from *@pisces* suggesting he or she might have known the victim.

Iris picked up her phone again and made a voice call to Elvis Chen, her former student and present IT consultant.

"Hey, Professor Reid. How's the new office? Is the network behaving?"

"Everything's fine here, but I have a question for you about Twitter. Do you know how to track down someone from a tweet?"

"Uh, this would be for a legit purpose, right? You're not stalking anyone?"

"My purpose is virtuous. I promise."

"Okay, in that case, depends on how often they've tweeted or posted any pictures. I might be able to pull GPS metadata from that to figure out where they are. And if there are a lot of pictures, I can use all the data to see where they tend to hang out. And if there's a selfie, well, I can use facial recognition to nail them. There are other tricks as well that I won't go into."

"And you don't need a subpoena for anything?"

Iris thought she could hear Elvis chuckling.

29

Later that afternoon, Iris was on the phone with Alex Harcon, talking about the new security system to be installed at the museum when she noticed a call coming in from Elvis.

She could hardly hurry her major client off the phone, so she was relieved when he wound down the conversation by suggesting that his engineers call Milo to co-ordinate the details of the set up.

As soon as Iris ended that call, she phoned Elvis back. "Did you discover who *@pisces* is?"

"I found out where the tweet was sent from," Elvis explained. "But this person is not into posting any photos. Maybe they're old or something."

Since Iris had never ventured onto Twitter for any reason, she figured she must fall into Elvis's "old" category. "Where was the location?"

"Gong Cha. Ever heard of it?"

"Can't say I have. Please tell me the tweet wasn't posted from some far corner of Southeast Asia."

"Nope. Right here in Harvard Square. It's a bubble tea place on Church Street. The best one around, IMHO."

"Is that all? He or she didn't post any pictures?"

"No, but **@pisces** sent another post last year besides the **good guy Sam** tweet. I'll text you a screenshot. It's a flyer about a soup kitchen open on Tuesday nights at the Unitarian church. The one at the corner of Mass Ave and Church Street, right in the Square. That tweet was sent from the church."

"A soup kitchen? Could **@pisces** volunteer there? Or maybe he's homeless? Both tweets were sent from Church Street. There's not much residential housing around there except the Harvard dorms, but he might work in the area. And he remembers a person from twenty years ago, so he has to be older than thirty."

"Or 'he' could be a 'she'."

"True. Drinking bubble tea seems like a girly thing, right?"

"*I* drink bubble tea," Elvis objected.

"Oops, sorry. This is helpful. Thanks. Go ahead and put your time on my tab."

"You have a tab?"

Iris shook off the comment and thought about what she had just learned. She figured the police wouldn't be able to get this level of information for several days. She was pretty sure that Elvis had found **@pisces**'s IP address by hacking into Twitter, so she couldn't exactly share the information with Lieutenant Garcia.

Her next call was to Ellie. "What's bubble tea?" Iris asked her friend.

"It's tea with tapioca balls in it. Raven says it's a big deal now. Why?"

"Someone sent a Tweet about our mystery skeleton from a bubble tea place in the Square. If I can find that person and learn who the victim was, maybe I can figure out who attacked Carl when they broke into our building to retrieve the remains."

"How is Carl doing?"

"He had a brain hemorrhage last night, and it doesn't look like he's going to make it. Milo's really cut up over it."

"Sounds like time to do surveillance at the tea shop. We need to track down the bastard and make him pay for what he did to Carl."

30

Iris met Ellie at the loft, and they walked along Mass Ave toward Harvard Square.

"What do you know about this tweeter?" Ellie asked.

"Not much. It could be a man or a woman. Over thirty. He or she used the tea shop's Wi-Fi to send a tweet responding to the story about the human remains." Iris showed Ellie a screenshot on her phone: **my friend sam a good guy.**

"The poster used a period at the end of a sentence? Definitely over thirty."

"This same person also posted a year ago about the soup kitchen at the First Parish church."

"Sent from the same tea shop IP address?"

"No." Iris stopped abruptly in the middle of the brick sidewalk. She couldn't believe she'd missed the obvious clue. "That one actually used the church's Wi-Fi."

Ellie raised an eyebrow. "Who has access to their Wi-Fi password?"

"Let's find out. We can stop there after the tea shop. But we have to be careful not to scare this possible source. I get the sense they're trying to stay under the radar."

"Why? If they know something about an old murder case, why not just come forward?"

"That's what we need to find out. Maybe they have some reason to steer clear of the police."

Iris and Ellie reached the First Parish Unitarian Church on the corner and turned onto Church Street. They noticed a small, yellowed sign on the church's side door fluttering in the breeze. Up close, they could make out the announcement of the soup kitchen being open that same night.

In the next half block, they passed two bookstores and two ice cream shops before arriving at the concrete and glass façade of the tea shop. It was 5:30, and workers were streaming out of their offices, heading for home. A few were ducking into Gong Cha.

Iris looked at Ellie and asked, "Have you been here before?"

"Not to this one. Raven took me to a different branch in Providence. They have franchises all over the world now, but they started in Taiwan."

Iris was struck by how tiny the place was. There were eight stools lined up against a counter which spanned the front window. Three of the seats were occupied by young people reading their phones or taking Instagram photos of their bubble tea. Six more patrons were lined up, waiting to order.

"Well, he or she isn't here," Ellie announced.

"How can you tell?"

"No one is close to the right age. Everyone here looks like a student or an entry-level office worker."

"You're right. I'm going to talk to the cashier. I'd better order something. What would you like? My treat."

Ellie shook her head. "I'm just here for my investigative skills."

"You don't like bubble tea?"

"It's something every open-minded person should try once, but I'm good."

"I love Asian food. I bet it will be good." Iris tried to figure out the complicated, lavishly illustrated menu on the wall. There were at least twice as many choices as Starbucks. When she reached the front of the line, she chose the picture that looked the most appealing. "Pearl Milk tea, please."

"What percent sugar and ice?" asked the cashier, a young Asian man with blue glasses.

"Whatever is most popular."

"30% milk, light ice?"

"Fine." Iris handed over her credit card. "By the way, do you give out the Wi-Fi password here?"

The cashier pointed to a sign on the wall which revealed it to be Bobateayum.

"Do you have many patrons other than students, maybe older ones?"

The cashier gave her a strange look. "Some."

"Any regulars?"

"No." He turned to the next woman in line. "Your order?"

Iris carried her plastic cup with its sealed foil top to the stool next to where Ellie waited. Dozens of brownish spheres the size of peas bobbed around in the top of her milky tea.

Ellie took the fat straw provided and pushed it through the foil top for her. "Enjoy."

Iris took a sip and sucked in several gooey balls. She chewed them, then tried to swallow. They got caught in her throat and she started gagging. She couldn't breathe.

Ellie pounded on Iris's back until she gulped down the gelatinous mass. She coughed a few times. When Iris was able to speak, she croaked, "I think I'm more of a coffee person."

"Time to go?"

Iris did a final 360 scan of the room, not spotting any candidates that might be ***@pisces***.

She tried to slide her almost-full cup discretely into the bin on the way out.

31

Iris and Ellie retraced their steps to the First Parish Church. A line of people snaked out the side door onto the sidewalk.

As they approached the building, Ellie whispered, "Should we wait in this line? It's really long."

"Sure. We want to talk to people. This gives us an opening." They took their place behind an elderly woman with flyaway silver hair and red capillaries spider-webbing across her nose and cheeks. She clutched several large bags tightly.

Iris gave the woman a smile. "Have you been coming here for a long time?"

The woman startled and turned to check out Iris before speaking. Her eyes drifted from Iris's clean hair to her small purse.

"You don't look like you need a free meal."

"We're here to see about volunteering," Iris improvised. "Do you know who we should speak with?"

The woman poked her chin suspiciously over at Ellie. "Her too?"

"Yes, we both want to learn about the program," Ellie said. "I'm Ellie and this is Iris. What's your name?"

The woman took a moment to respond. "Freida."

Iris held out her hand to shake. "Nice to meet you."

Freida reluctantly shook both of their hands, then wiped them on her long skirt. "Judith."

Iris and Ellie waited for an explanation.

"She's in charge of the volunteers. Talk to her." At that point, Freida seemed to make a decision. She grabbed Iris by the elbow and called over her shoulder for Ellie to follow them. Freida pushed past the rest of the people in line, whacking them with her bags, as she called out loudly, "new volunteers coming through."

Dozens of pairs of eyes: some angry, some placid, some seemingly deranged, followed the progress of the three women through the red entrance door, through a vestibule and into a big room on the left. Inside, a long table was crowded with platters of lasagna, a vat of soup, sandwiches, fruit, and cookies. A nearby round table held carafes of coffee, hot chocolate and juices, with tottering stacks of paper cups. People were loading up their plates and moving along into another room at the far end, from which came the sound of shouting and laughter. The view through a small window in a second door suggested a kitchen.

There must have been nearly a hundred people moving through the rooms. Iris tried to decipher ages of the diners. More than half were over thirty. How could she and Ellie figure out who had sent that Tweet?

Freida steered them over to a woman ladling out soup. "I brought you two new volunteers, Judith."

"Why, thank you Freida." A tall, middle-aged woman with frizzy brown hair dragged back into a ponytail beamed at Iris and Ellie expectantly. She handed her ladle over to a woman standing next to her and extended her hand to Iris.

"I'm Iris and this is my friend Ellie. We read in the *Cambridge Chronicle* about the great work you're doing down here."

"Oh, did they write about us again?" Judith smiled.

"The article might have been a while ago, but I saved it."

Ellie spoke up. "Have you been running the soup kitchen for a long time?"

"I've been volunteering here for about fifteen years. The program started in the 1980s when homelessness became a major problem, though it's nothing new. We get runaways, the mentally challenged, people who've been priced out of their apartments, all sorts. This is a place where everyone is treated with dignity."

"That's so important. Are there other volunteers who've also been helping out here a long time?"

Judith looked around. "A lot of the student volunteers come and go. And occasionally some local residents help out, especially around Thanksgiving. But I guess I'm the only old timer who holds it together."

"Ellie and I were wondering if we might do a food drive in our Avon Hill neighborhood for your pantry. Would that be helpful?"

Judith considered. "We don't have a lot of storage space here at the church, but if I gave you a list of the specific things we need, that would be a lovely idea. And some donors might want to contribute cash or gift cards for our homeless guests instead. That's always appreciated."

Iris noticed a young volunteer carrying Freida's bags for her as the older woman brought her full plate into the dining area. A few of the diners were looking at their phones.

"Would cell phones be a useful gift for your guests—simple prepaid phones? Do you offer Wi-Fi service in the church?"

Judith looked pleased at this idea. "Yes, phones would be welcome. We do give out our password. But our guests can only use it on Tuesday evenings when they're here for the soup kitchen. We change it every week."

Iris remembered that the tweet about Sam had been posted yesterday, on a Monday.

"I'm actually in this area a lot. I'm working as the architect for a building on Mount Auburn Street. We're turning it into a museum."

Judith cocked her head. "I think I've heard about that project. Didn't you have a break-in recently?"

"We did. And one of our construction crewmembers was attacked."

"I saw that on the news. I'm so sorry."

"We also discovered human remains that had been hidden on our site a long time ago."

Judith's eyebrows rose.

"The police think the two things might be connected," Iris said.

Judith gave her a stern look. "I think you two better come back to my office."

32

Iris and Ellie followed Judith back past the vestibule and through another door into a small, wood-paneled room.

"This is Reverend Casey's office, but she lets me use it when she's not here. Have a seat." Judith gestured to the two chairs across from a heavy desk as she sat down behind it. "Why are you really here?"

Iris became aware of the loud ticking of an analog clock on the desk. "As I mentioned, our head carpenter was hurt very badly and probably won't make it through the night. We think that the person who assaulted him is connected to a murder from twenty years ago. Someone sent a tweet from this church suggesting that they might know who the previous victim was. Did you send it?"

Ellie added, "We're not the police. We just want to find whoever beat Carl up with a crowbar. Maybe we can get justice for both of these victims."

Judith winced. "And you think that finding out the identity of the first victim from two decades ago will be enough to point you to the person behind his assault?"

"It's not much to go on, but it's our only lead," Iris admitted. "We're pretty sure the assailant was trying to retrieve evidence of the earlier crime when he encountered Carl. If we can learn something about the first victim, we might be able to figure out why someone killed him, and that could lead us to Carl's attacker."

The clock's rhythmic beats filled the silence. Finally, Judith spoke. "The police didn't seem interested at the time."

"We're interested." Ellie's voice was gentle. "Tell us about Sam."

"Twenty years ago, I was living on the streets with a nineteen-year-old boy named Sam Parker. After I ran away from home, I saw him busking in Harvard Square. He was really good. He could sing and play anything, but mainly rock and roll. Sam was a gentle soul. He wrote songs and poetry. We decided to team up. I would harmonize with him and pass the hat. He wasn't interested in me romantically, to my chagrin. We were just two runaways trying to protect each other from a tough life."

A tear rolled slowly down Judith's cheek. "We were doing okay through the summer. The tourists were generous. We'd sleep down by the river. But then, in the fall, it started to get cold. We didn't want to go to a shelter. We got low on money and didn't have enough to eat. Sam had this idea about selling weed to the students. He knew a dealer in East Cambridge and said it would be easy money. By that point, we were hungry and desperate."

Tears rolled freely down her cheeks now. "Then one night in October, we were hanging out in Harvard Square, and Sam was dealing. It had gotten dark, and I curled up in my sleeping bag and fell asleep. When I woke up, Sam had vanished. An old guy who was a regular told me Sam had been in a fight and three guys had hauled him off. I waited all day for him to return. No one had seen him. The next day, I went to the police and tried to file a missing person report, but the cops had no interest. They said Sam wasn't a minor, and I wasn't a family member."

Ellie shook her head in disbelief. "They never filled out any paperwork about his disappearance?"

"No. He wasn't worth their time. Sam was a street person, a

runaway. Things have gotten a bit more enlightened now." Judith shrugged. "At least on the surface."

"Did Sam have a family? Did you ever try to contact them after he disappeared?"

"They live somewhere in the Midwest. Sam told me they disowned him after he came out as gay. He wanted nothing to do with them."

Iris bit her lip. A moment later she asked, "How soon after that did you get yourself off the streets?"

"I waited a month for Sam to come back, then I crawled back home, tail between my legs. I couldn't take the life anymore. But that's why I volunteer here now. I have a good day job, a decent place to live. And I do what I can to help those people out there." She nodded toward the door.

The three women were silent for a few moments. Then, Ellie asked, "Did you get any description of the three students who took Sam away?"

"The old guy just said they looked like students. Jackass students, he called them."

"I don't suppose you're still in touch with this old guy?"

"He's long gone." Judith stood, a clear sign that the discussion was over. "I don't know if Sam is the one who was buried in your building, but the timing and location sure fit."

33

An hour later, the two women were back at Iris's loft, assembling an impromptu dinner. Rock riffs from Tash Sultana's new album filled the kitchen, and the women harmonized and wiggled their hips to the heavy bass. Ellie stood beside her chopping green peppers to the beat of the music while Iris tossed several cut-up cucumbers into a blender and punched the puree button. Sheba snorted, got up from the kitchen floor, and trudged into the living room to escape the mechanical grinding noise.

Iris collected four plump, red tomatoes from the windowsill and handed them to Ellie. "Here. Chop these while I mince the garlic."

Ellie set down her wine glass. "I can't believe you still have tomatoes from your garden."

"These are the last of them. They're not as intense as the ones last month, but they're fine for gazpacho."

Ellie picked up the knife. "I don't think I've ever been here while the restaurant was operating. Is Luc going to run up the staircase and tell us to be quiet so we won't disturb his customers?"

"It wouldn't be him. He'd send a busboy, er, bus person. At this hour, Luc's in a cooking frenzy." Iris wrapped a fresh sourdough baguette in aluminum foil and edged it into the oven. "But don't worry. I made sure Milo thoroughly soundproofed the restaurant ceiling during the renovation."

"Have you heard from Milo recently about how Carl is doing?"

"I should call him." She deposited the big bowl of soup into the refrigerator and handed Ellie the half-empty bottle of Sauvignon Blanc. "Let's move to the living room and give the gazpacho a chance to chill."

They joined Sheba on the sofa, and Iris fumbled for her phone in the pocket of her jeans.

When Milo answered her question, his voice was clearly strained. "Carl didn't make it. He passed this afternoon. I meant to call but I've been busy helping Gail make the arrangements. Sorry, I've got to go."

Iris stared down at the silent phone in her hand, slack-mouthed.

Ellie watched her. "What? Carl is dead?"

Iris nodded. "Oh, God. I should call his wife, send food, flowers… something. But Milo hung up. They're busy now."

Ellie put a hand on Iris's shoulder. "Give them some time. Then you can ask how you can help."

As Iris thought about it, maybe the best way she could help would be to find the jackass students who'd dragged away Sam Parker twenty years ago. That might lead to capturing Carl's killer.

34

Iris woke up early the next morning with a free-floating sense of dread. She covered her eyes with her hand and tried to remember why. The strong aroma of coffee filled the room, and when she opened her eyes, she saw Luc sitting on the edge of the bed, worry etched across his forehead. He held a steaming cup of something light-brown and frothy. "Double latte." He handed it to her. "You were crying out in your sleep all night. I tried to wake you, but it kept happening."

Then Iris remembered that Carl was dead—beaten to death with a crowbar on *her* job site. And on top of that, years before, someone had brutally smashed gentle Sam Parker's hands before murdering him, probably in the same location.

"What is it?" Luc asked. "Did something bad happen at work yesterday?"

She downed the latte in two throat-searing gulps, coughed hard, then blurted out the whole story.

Luc tenderly smoothed the hair back from her forehead and hugged her. "Come here. It's okay. It's going to be okay. Do you want me to stay with you today? I can have Arnold sub for me tonight."

Iris pulled back enough to see him. Coming from any serious chef, this was a big offer. She realized, at that moment, she'd never loved anyone more. The thought of staying home cocooned with him was tempting. She gave him a long, lingering kiss. Then, reluctantly, she murmured, "Thanks, babe. I'd love to cancel a meeting I have this morning, but I should probably focus on work."

"Are you sure? You can call me later if you change your mind." Luc ran his hands up and down her arms. "Why don't you take a walk with Sheba around Fresh Pond before you head into the office? It's nice and warm out. You can clear your head."

Iris felt a balmy breeze fluttering the curtains through the open bedroom windows. "Maybe I will."

The whole of Massachusetts was seized by a post summer heat wave. Iris and Sheba started around the main path of the 162-acre park encircling the city's reservoir. It was 8:30 in the morning, and a pre-work crowd of runners, cyclists, and dog walkers all vied for space on the tree-shaded dirt walkway. Iris breathed in deeply. She could hear the distant static roar of cars around the park's periphery and overhead a plane on the Logan approach was briefly visible below the clouds. But this sun-dappled piece of land was a secret paradise hidden in the middle of a crowded city.

Iris slipped an elastic off her wrist and pulled her hair back into a ponytail. "Ready, Sheba? Time to pick up the pace." Her stubby-legged Basset hound looked up at her doubtfully, ears drooping on the ground. Iris broke into a jog, and her long-suffering dog managed to keep up. They dodged around a speed-walker who was declaiming into her Bluetooth at considerable volume that she was married to a stale ham sandwich of a human.

When they were half-way around the two-and-a-quarter-mile loop, Iris slowed down in deference to Sheba's short legs and flagging pace. She sat down on a bench and watched a formation of Canada geese soar just above the trees, honking obnoxiously.

A dozen boys of various teenage sizes and shapes ran by, wearing the sleek shorts and matching T-shirts of their school's cross-country team. Iris's gaze was drawn to their quickly receding backs. She felt something tickle her memory.

It took a moment before she realized why. Their uniforms were precisely the shade between Aegean blue and Mediterranean blue on the Pantone color chart.

35

From the G & B logo on the back of the runners' uniforms, Iris realized that this distinctive blue was the school color of the Gorgas and Blanker School in Cambridge. As soon as Iris finished her loop around the Fresh Pond Reservoir, she hoisted Sheba into the car and drove to Upland Road, the street adjacent to the family home she'd sold the year before. Her neighbor, Alise, had taught math at that private school for many years before she retired. Raven and her friends who'd attended the public high school referred to the G & B kids as Gorgons and Wankers.

More significantly, Iris was certain that the G & B school blue matched the scrap of material which the police had recovered from between the floor joists where Sam Parker's remains had been stashed. Judith had reported that the three "jackass students" who'd been buying weed from Sam Parker those many years ago had scuffled with him and then dragged him away from the center of Harvard Square. Iris assumed that the students were college-aged, given how many there were in the area. But what if they were high-school kids, and the material was snagged from something one of them was wearing? Sam was a small guy, and any number of older teenagers could have overpowered him, especially with three of them versus one of him.

After Iris finished parking her Tesla in front of Alise's small Victorian house, she conjured up an image of the gym uniform color juxtaposed against the scrap of material from the building site. She had almost perfect color memory and they seemed identical. But she still wanted to see the G & B school blue up close. Alise must have some school-branded article of clothing from her years teaching there.

Iris helped Sheba out of the car. The dog was wriggling with excitement to see her old dog-sitter again, and she waddled quickly up the walkway. When Iris pulled the knob of the old-fashioned doorbell, she was relieved to hear someone moving around inside. She should have called first.

Alise greeted them with hugs. She wore her hair in a gray braid down her back, which swung like a horse's tail as Iris followed her to the sunny kitchen at the rear of the house. After Alise treated Sheba to several biscuits, and the dog lay contentedly at her feet, Iris explained why she'd stopped by.

Alise listened carefully as she put a kettle on the stove. "I saw on the news about the bones discovered in Harvard Square and wondered if it happened in your museum building. You really think whoever killed that boy all those years ago might have been a student at Gorgas and Blanker? I was teaching there then. If you're right, I might well have known the student."

While Alise seemed surprised by the idea, she didn't seem disbelieving.

"Am I off base here?" Iris asked. "I heard about three young men who bought weed in Harvard Square from Sam, the boy who was killed. One of them got into a mix-up with Sam and then the bunch of them dragged him away."

"There are some tough cookies at G & B. And we know that anyone can kill, even young kids. The teen years are especially brutal. And the girls can be worse than the boys. Most schools have bullies, and sometimes they attract a posse who carries out the alpha dog's dirty work. The dynamic in any high school can be straight out of 'Lord of the Flies.'"

Iris nodded solemnly. She remembered her own high school years. Then she refocused on the purpose for her visit. "Some material in the exact shade of G & B blue got snagged on a nail on the side of the floor joists where Sam's body was hidden. That's what makes me think the trio may have been students back then. The scrap might have come from track pants or gym shorts, or the sleeve of a windbreaker. It looked shiny. Has the school always had those colors? What blue articles of clothing did the boys usually wear?"

Alise poured hot water over tea bags in a pair of mugs as she considered the question. "Their school uniforms are navy blazers and khakis, but the ties are that particular blue. However, the boys whip those off the minute they leave school property, especially if they're venturing into Harvard Square. Still, they might wear something with that blue from an after-school sport. It's been the school color for as long as I remember. I have an old yearbook somewhere from when the headmaster asked me to be a substitute advisor for the yearbook committee, but it's nowhere near twenty years old. Hold on a second."

She reappeared a few minutes later, holding a large volume, and handed it to Iris. "Look at the team photos in the back. The pictures are black and white, but you can get a sense of what they were wearing."

Iris leafed through the thick, shiny yearbook pages. The various teams wore gym shorts, track pants and windbreakers in a color that looked gray in the photographs but was probably blue. She supposed that the Gorgas and Blanker school library would have yearbooks from twenty years ago, but even if Alise could get them for her, how would looking through them tell Iris anything? Would some boy have a malevolent look that telegraphed 'killer'? "I don't suppose you remember any boys from that era who struck you as having particularly violent tendencies?"

"Too many to single out just one. Do you know which year the three students might have graduated?"

Good question. Iris was silent for a few moments, making mental calculations. "Between the Medical Examiner's estimate based on Sam's remains and the date when Sam's friend said he went missing, we think that he was killed around October 2003. So, I'd imagine the students would be class of '04, '05, or possibly '06."

"Let's see. Approximately sixty students per year in each class, with half male, so you'd have a maximum of ninety possible suspects."

"I forgot you used to be a math teacher."

Alise smiled. "Depending on whether brute force was used, you can probably eliminate the smaller, slighter boys. Then again if there were three of them...I'd need to refresh my memory about who the students were during those years."

Iris carried her empty mug to the sink. "Do you have anything from the school in that blue color for comparison with the sample from our building site?"

Alise tilted her head. "I was given a scarf in the school colors when I retired. I don't like scarves and I've never worn it. Let me get it." She went upstairs and returned a few minutes later. "You're welcome to keep it."

As Iris expected, the color of the scarf was the exact shade she remembered.

36

Iris barely had time to drive to her office and get settled before her 10:00 clients arrived. She was relieved that Rollo had thought ahead and pinned up prints of the house plans and elevations on the conference room wall. He had left his laptop angled to project more images onto an adjacent wall.

She led Sheba into her office and tossed a rawhide bone from the desk drawer onto the dog's bed. "Make it last for an hour. At least." Sheba responded to the instructions with her best long-suffering look.

Iris slipped into her seat at the head of the gleaming, brand-new conference table minutes before Loretta led her clients back through the open office to meet her. The welcome aroma of coffee emanated from a silver Georg Jensen carafe on the credenza along the side wall. Fresh muffins from the nearby Hi-Rise Bakery were arranged on a platter on top of the new walnut cabinet. Iris shifted into hostess mode and made a mental note to give Loretta a raise. After a few words of greeting, she introduced Rollo, who wore a jacket and tie for his role as the Project Architect.

Rollo guided the husband and wife through a 3-D tour as he described what their home would look like after the renovation. Iris swiveled slightly in her ergonomic chair, her mind drifting to thoughts of Milo and how he was handling Carl's death. She needed to call him as soon as the meeting was over.

The clients asked some thoughtful questions. An hour after the meeting began, they rose to leave, the husband holding a roll of the newest blackline design drawings.

After they were out of sight, Iris gave Rollo a high-five. "Not bad for your first big-time client meeting. How did it feel?"

"Wow. Could you tell I was nervous?"

"Not at all," she lied. Rollo had been sweating bullets and practically vibrating through the whole meeting, but he had done well.

Once Iris retreated to her office, she punched in Milo's number on her phone, but the call went straight to voicemail. As she disconnected, she spotted Alise's blue scarf trailing out the corner of her tote bag. She needed to get in touch with Lieutenant Garcia ASAP. She should have called him yesterday after her eye-opening visit to the soup kitchen.

As soon as Iris got through and told him she had found someone who might have known the victim from twenty years ago, Garcia wanted to know how she'd managed to locate this person.

"I saw a woman leaving flowers outside the door to our building project and I went over and talked to her," Iris improvised. "She was living on the streets back then and her nineteen-year-old friend, Sam Parker, disappeared from Harvard Square one night. She tried to file a missing-person report with the police, but they told her he wasn't a minor, so they wouldn't bother to file any paperwork."

Iris thought she heard Garcia swear under his breath.

"Sam Parker was his name?"

"That's what she said he went by."

"So, she left the tweet?"

"Yes."

"How can I get in touch with her?"

"I don't think she wants to talk to the authorities, but I can give her your number and maybe she'll call you."

"Ms. Reid. Carl Nowak has died and now we're trying to find out who killed him. We believe his assailant was in the building to retrieve someone's remains when the attack occurred. I hope you are not trying to obstruct our investigation…"

"I wouldn't be calling you if I wasn't trying to help. Carl Nowak was the head carpenter on my project. Of course, I want his murderer found. I'll give the woman I met your phone number and say that you'd like her to call. That's all I can promise. I've already given you Sam Parker's name. His family was from the Midwest and disowned him because he was gay. Now would you like to hear about an interesting, related discovery?"

Iris definitely heard a snort from the other end of the line.

She continued, "That material you found in the niche with Sam's remains?"

"Sam's alleged remains."

"I believe that exact blue is the school color for the Gorgas and Blanker School in Cambridge. I have a scarf here that a former teacher gave me in that very distinctive hue. Would you like me to drop it by your office?"

There was a moment of silence. Garcia's voice sounded of exaggerated patience. "As soon as possible."

37

No sooner had Iris set her phone down after the call with Lieutenant Garcia than it buzzed like an angry hornet, walking itself across the desktop. She saw on its display that the caller was Alex Harcon, so she grabbed it.

"Hi, Alex. How are you?"

"Iris, good morning. My media people informed me that the carpenter on Milo's crew died yesterday."

"Yes. Milo told me last night. A blood vessel in Carl's brain burst. I was just about to call you."

After a brief silence, Alex said, "I'm sorry to hear that. Would you please get me his wife's contact information? I'd like to offer my condolences."

"Of course."

"I'll call Milo as well. How is he holding up?"

"As well as can be expected. They were friends. He's helping Gail to plan the funeral."

"Tragic thing. It should never have happened." Iris heard Alex say a few words *sotto voce* to someone in his office before continuing back with her. "Have you seen all these recent tweets? They're calling my building a 'museum of horrors'."

"That will blow over. Social media always moves on quickly to the next tragedy. Would you like me to see if Nili can help with controlling the publicity? Maybe he can have his assistant post some counter-tweets to make the history of the building sound exciting." She wavered in mid-thought as she remembered how the two victims had met their ends.

"Good idea. Why don't you give Nili a call and suggest that?"

After ending the call, Iris felt a definite need to comfort Milo. Would he be at the job site today? She decided to go look for him there, since he hadn't returned her call.

She left Sheba with Loretta and headed outside to her car. Taking a loop out of her way, Iris stopped at Police Headquarters in East Cambridge. She dropped off a manila envelope for Lieutenant Garcia containing the scarf at the bullet-proof service window in the lobby.

Her next challenge was to find a legal parking space in Harvard Square, always difficult. Luckily, she was able to swoop into a metered space that an enormous SUV had just vacated. She paid the parking fee on her phone app and walked three blocks to her building.

Milo was kneeling on the floor, wearing headphones and incising grooves into the subfloor. Dewey stood nearby, cutting planks of wood into what were probably stair treads on a table saw. The arc of the free-standing, curved staircase was laid out on the subfloor in pencil, following the alignment from her construction drawings. She moved in front of Milo. He glanced up and switched off the router, signaling Dewey to turn off his noisy saw too, so they could talk.

Iris sat down on the dusty floor and studied Milo for some insight into his state of mind, but he seemed altogether focused on the task at hand. "You're going with the stilt approach instead of the cage?" Even though Iris had drawn all the plans, sections, and elevations for the complex staircase, she'd left it up to him to decide which way to build it.

"Yeah, I've built one this way before, so I figured I'd stick with the devil I know. So, when's the film crew coming back?"

"Forget the film crew. They can wait. Why don't you close down the job for a few days? Take some time to process what happened. You and the crew. There's no hard deadline on this project."

Milo rocked back on his heels. "Yeah. Maybe I should do that. Thanks for the suggestion. There's going to be a memorial service for Carl on Saturday at 10:00. I hope you can make it. It will be at the Stanton Funeral Home in Watertown. Just past the Star Market on Mount Auburn."

"Uh, huh. Anything I can do to help? Harcon wants to send flowers."

"Gail and I have it under control. The construction crew is meeting here beforehand, and we'll ride our motorcycles over there in formation. Carl would have liked a send-off like that."

38

Jim liked Nashville. He soaked up the afternoon sun while lounging on a bench in Centennial Park, overlooking a full-sized replica of the Parthenon which some former Tennessean had decided belonged there. It was sixty degrees in October, the people were friendly, the food was great, and he could listen to live music in a different honky-tonk bar every night of the week. Even the attractive local women down here didn't seem to mind a few extra pounds on a middle-aged guy.

Jim had found a cheap studio near downtown, which he'd rented with cash for a month. And there were ways to pass the time during this forced exile: he could take in a Titans football game at Nissan Stadium, visit the Johnny Cash Museum, or catch Country Music acts at the Grande Ole Opry, to name some. But all he could think about was how much he'd rather be seeing these places with Jimmy Jr.

If anyone wanted to know, he was calling himself Jamie Peterson, a luxury car dealer from Providence, R.I. on vacation here for an unspecified amount of time. He'd have to be vague about his plans because he wasn't sure how long he'd need to stay in hiding. An article on the *Globe.com* website said that the police now knew about that kid's bones under the floorboards, but would the cops figure out who had killed him and put him there so long ago? He and Trent were the two surviving witnesses, and Trent sure as hell wasn't going to tell. As for the lumberjack's death, that was more recent, so probably a greater danger. The CSI TV shows made it look like the cops could track down bad guys from a speck of DNA left behind at a crime scene or even a thread from their clothes.

Was he a bad guy? He'd certainly gone along with a very rotten thing twenty years ago. And now he was hiding from both the police and from Trent. Good guys didn't find themselves in this position, did they? But Trent was the real barracuda. Jim was just a minnow. Could he possibly trade immunity for revealing what he knew about Trent. But who would he tell?

39

Trent could not believe that Jim Dugan had managed to elude a predator like Edward Weber. He almost had to admire his old high-school buddy who'd managed to stay off the grid for four days now. Jimbo didn't use any credit cards or contact the ex-wife or kid. He hadn't applied for a job at a golf club anywhere in the country, or any other position requiring a real Social Security number. But he'd screw up sooner or later.

Edward sat on the other side of the large desk in Trent's office at campaign HQ, the door locked, looking as uncomfortable as Trent had ever seen him. Which meant that the former Army Ranger was drumming one finger against the side of the leather visitor's armchair.

Trent stroked his receding chin. "Tell me about the last sighting."

"Mr. Dugan abandoned his car at Logan Airport, obviously a ruse. We caught him on a surveillance camera at South Station, heading for the Amtrak platform. There were two trains leaving around that time, one headed for Chicago, one for Washington, D.C. I'm sorry to say, sir, that we lost him at this point. We don't know which train he got on."

"So, Jim could be anywhere in the country, maybe even the

world, possessing information that could be highly detrimental to my campaign."

"I've been working all my sources, and I doubt that he could have made it over the border without showing his passport. Or slipped through any of the porous sections."

"Even so, that leaves forty-eight states he could be hiding in. How about a boat? Could he have sailed to Bermuda, or someplace like that? Then island-hopped away?"

"I have sources at the most likely ports. Nobody has seen him."

"What about the less likely ports? I think we are finding that Mr. Dugan may just be craftier than we expected."

"We do have the leverage we discussed, sir."

Trent raised an eyebrow. "Ah, yes. Jimmy Jr. The nuclear option."

Edward maintained an opaque expression. "Yes, sir. I imagine that would draw Dugan back."

"Risky, though. It could get the FBI involved."

Edward gave a tiny shrug. "The ball's in your court."

"Let's give it a few more days. But I can't wait too long. The election's in a few weeks and any adverse press this late in the campaign… Well, I don't have to tell you."

"No sir, you don't."

40

By Saturday, the weather had turned. The last gasps of summer gave way to a brisk autumn chill. Shivering, Iris got out of bed and shut the bedroom windows. *Why is Luc never cold?* She changed from her silk nightshirt into a long-sleeved navy dress for Carl's memorial service.

Luc was already up, humming to himself in the kitchen while expertly flipping pancakes. He glanced over his shoulder. "I can go with you if you want."

"Thanks, but that's okay. I'm not planning on staying long." Iris fixed herself an espresso and filled the rest of the cup with warm milk. "I worked with Carl on the restaurant project and Ash's art studio, but I didn't really know him well. We mainly communicated through Milo."

"And I know Milo from the Paradise renovation. Which one was Carl?"

"He was the big guy with the red beard. Which doesn't narrow it down much. All of Milo's workers resemble Vikings. Milo, at five foot ten, is the shrimp in the group. But they all look up to him. And they all seem to ride motorcycles."

Luc frowned. "Are they Hell's Angels?"

"No, but Milo said they belong to some special motorcycle club for people in the construction trades."

Luc handed Iris a warm plate of pancakes and a hopeful Sheba followed her to the dining table.

Iris easily found the white clapboard building that housed the Stanton Funeral Home. It was conveniently located next to the Sacred Heart Church, but Milo hadn't mentioned anything about a religious service. She parked in the lot and noticed a large number of big, low-slung motorcycles lined up in an orderly row.

Around front, the main entry had double doors, which caused Iris to envision caskets rolling in and out to waiting hearses—always thinking like a practical architect, even at a time like this. A sign in the hall directed her to the Willow Room on the left, but Iris had merely to follow the crowd. The room was packed, and all the metal folding chairs were taken. She joined the late comers standing in the rear and looked around for Milo.

A large color photo of Carl was displayed on an easel at the front of the room. He was sitting on an enormous motorcycle, undoubtedly a Harley Davidson, and smiling broadly. He looked full of energy and enthusiasm for life. Iris shifted her weight, suddenly overcome with sadness. The guy should still be alive, dammit.

Instead of a coffin, a large gray urn sat on a table beside the easel. An enormous wreath of white lilies, which Iris guessed was from Alex Harcon, rested against the table leg. The strong scent reached Iris at the back of the room.

Iris spotted Gail Nowak in the front row and thought about how awful the woman must feel to know that Carl had died in part because she'd kicked him out after a fight. Her black shirt and pants gave her skin a sallow cast and she looked numb. Milo sat next to her in the same suit he'd worn to the art studio opening. He wore his black hair in a single braid down his back and his expression was desolate.

Iris observed the attendees from her vantage spot at the back of the room. Dewey and the other carpenters were sitting in the row behind Milo. She noticed that many in the audience, mostly men but a few women as well, wore jackets that identified their companies: Maloney Electric, Nunez Plasterers, Sobieski Plumbing and Heating. She guessed they were members of Carl's motorcycle club.

At precisely 10:00, Milo stood, holding a piece of paper, strode over to the portrait of Carl, and turned to face the crowd. He welcomed everyone and read a poem by Mary Oliver called *When Death Comes*. By the end, there were sniffles and eye-wipings throughout the audience.

The next few speakers told stories about Carl as a friend or co-worker. Carl's brother, another large red-headed man, finished up the sequence of eulogies with several funny anecdotes about Carl as a boy. Gail stayed in her seat and didn't speak.

Finally, Milo stood up again and announced that anyone who wanted to join him could follow along to the Ridgelawn Cemetery, about fifteen minutes away, where Carl's cremains would be placed in a family crypt. He would lead the motorcycles first and the cars could follow behind. The funeral home attendants would hand out flags with magnetic bases to attach to the vehicles in the procession.

Eric Clapton's song "Tears in Heaven" played over the sound system as the guests filed out. Iris ran into Dewey in the hall, and he told her that Milo's band was playing a tribute concert for Carl that evening and gave her the details. By the time Iris made it back to her car, the motorcycles were lined up in the driveway, with Milo in the lead. He circled a finger overhead and the riders behind him started their engines. A police car halted traffic as Milo led the somber procession slowly down Mount Auburn Street, picking up speed as the last of the cars fell in line.

41

When Iris returned home, instead of going upstairs to the loft, she opened the first-floor mudroom door to the restaurant kitchen. Luc was alone and looked up from a large pot of liquid he had simmering on the fancy Italian range. He adjusted the heat to low and moved over to meet her at the doorway. "You look sad. Come here."

She leaned against him and wrapped her arms around his waist. After a few moments, she pulled back, but held onto one of his hands. "God, Luc. Life can be so fragile. A stranger can just erase you from existence."

Luc squeezed her hand lightly. "That's why we need to appreciate what we have now." He swept her hair back from her face and leaned down to kiss her. "Let's do something tonight after the last seating. I would love to cut loose with you on a Saturday night for once."

"Well—Milo's band is playing at *the Plough and Stars*. I wonder how he'll be after all this."

"I haven't been to *the Plough* in ages. Let's go. They'll just be getting underway by 11:00. I'll have Arnold close up for me."

Iris skimmed her hand over his perfect butt before heading upstairs.

It was close to 11:30 by the time Iris and Luc parked and walked up to the tiny Irish bar outside of Cambridge's Central Square. As Luc held open the door for her, raucous music poured out to the sidewalk. The place was packed, standing room only.

Iris had never heard Milo's band play before. She knew it was called Ritual Magic from the band T-shirts the crew often wore. The music was a soulful rock, played at ear-splitting volume. Maybe she and Luc wouldn't stay long. They wedged themselves into a corner tucked in beside the front door.

Luc shouted to be heard. "What can I get you?"

"Double vodka, rocks with a lime. Thanks." Iris slipped off her suede jacket and draped it over her shoulder as she looked around. The walls were tomato red, and an actual plough hung above the bar. Giant rhinestone stars dangled from the ceiling. She could make out Milo on the small stage at the far end of the space, wearing his usual black leather pants, surrounded by his bandmates. She couldn't understand a single word of what he was singing. "Lousy acoustics," she muttered to herself.

Luc's blond head was visible against a sea of baseball caps surging its way toward one of the two overburdened bartenders. The song ended abruptly, and her ears rang in the quiet interlude before Milo's guitar resumed its pounding rhythm. The drummer picked up the beat and the bass player joined in. Two enormous amps were stacked up next to the poor keyboard player, who was probably deaf by now. Whatever he was singing about, Milo was getting very worked up. He was covered in sweat, and his long black hair was plastered to his back. At one point, she was certain that he was looking straight at her.

"Sorry, that took forever." Luc handed her a sweating glass of clear vodka, not much ice. He took a sip of what looked like a dark, intense beer. "Milo seems to have quite a following."

"Or else this is a typical Saturday night at *the Plough and Stars*. I haven't been here since architecture school."

"We used to sneak in with fake IDs when I was in high school, not that they were too particular back then."

Iris smiled, remembering some of her own high school exploits, and downed the rest of her vodka, leaving the ice cubes and the tiny slice of lime high and dry.

Milo launched into a less shouty, more danceable song. Luc set their empty glasses on the end of the bar and took Iris's hand. He started moving his hips, slowly at first, and she joined him. The room came alive as people swayed and tapped to the beat. The bass player's unexpected tenor harmonized well with Milo's baritone.

Iris felt the desolation of the day melt away.

The next song was a slow one. Iris placed a hand on Luc's shoulder, and he reached for her other hand. He spun her around, managing to avoid slamming her into the people tightly packed around them, then pulled her back into a tight clutch. Luc was a great dancer.

"We should do this more often." Luc spoke in her ear. "In fact, I've been thinking…"

Iris waited.

"There's something I've been wanting to ask you." He looked deadly serious.

She stopped dancing.

"But not here. It's too noisy."

Was he about to propose? She'd been fantasizing about this moment, not sure if she was ready for it, but wanting it, nevertheless. She told herself that, as a strong, independent woman, she didn't need to be married to feel whole. Still, she loved Luc and wanted to be reassured of his commitment to her.

Luc grabbed her hand and led her out into the chilly night toward the car.

Was he going to ask her in the car? Not very romantic.

"There's something at home I want to show you."

Oh, God. He must have already bought a ring. What if it was ugly? She'd have to keep a delighted expression on her face. They could exchange it later.

"Do I get any hints?"

Luc smiled as he opened the car door for her. He looked so handsome in the stark light of the oncoming traffic.

"I just hope you'll be as excited about it as I am," he started up the car.

Iris took some deep breaths. They'd been living together for a year. Almost to the day, now that she thought about it. That might account for Luc's timing. The guy could be very sentimental. Would she need to shift into wedding planning mode right away? Was Raven too old to be a flower girl? Ellie, once again, would be her matron-of-honor. Iris wondered how many guests would fit in the restaurant if they went with a buffet instead of sit-down service. And where should they go on their honeymoon? Did she ever tell Luc that, since her first honeymoon in St Barth's with Christopher, she detested beach vacations?

He parked behind the loft, and they sailed up the stairs. Iris felt herself tingling. She wanted to remember every detail about this moment. Sheba met her on the second floor and followed her around the living room as Iris turned on some of the table lights, setting the mood.

Luc disappeared into their bedroom. "I'll be right out."

Should she open some wine? Or that bottle of Krug champagne they were saving for a special occasion? No, let him suggest it. She arranged herself attractively on the sofa, butterflies skittering around in her stomach.

Luc returned a minute later, looking nervous and holding a rolled-up magazine in his hand. A *magazine*? He placed it on the coffee table in front of her and opened it to a page marked with a scrap of paper.

"I was reading *Food & Wine* and came across this article by a chef from Chicago. He talks about this awesome surf camp he went to in Costa Rica. By the end of two weeks, the dude was actually a decent surfer. What do you say?"

"About him becoming a decent surfer?"

"About us going to surf camp? We need a vacation!"

42

The previous night, Iris's disappointment about the lack of a proposal kept her tossing and turning. She bought herself some time by agreeing in principle to a vacation, but saying she needed to think about the surf camp idea.

The next morning, Iris and Luc slept in, then relaxed over coffee, eggs Florentine and the *Sunday Globe*. Iris made it halfway through the magazine crossword puzzle before Luc brought up surf camp again.

He was studying travel sites on his iPad. "This site says the best time to visit Costa Rica is November through March. When do you think you could take time off? Maybe after Christmas? That's always a slow time for business."

"Luc, I'm not really a beach person. I like more stuff to do, more stimulation. How about a trip to Paris? That would be romantic."

"Learning to surf would be stimulating. We'd leave the dark and cold of winter in Cambridge for sun, palm trees and a turquoise ocean. They make this drink called a Guaro Sour that you'd love. And the image of you rocking a tiny bikini and balancing on a surfboard..."

"Don't they have to wear wetsuits because the ocean is so cold?"

Luc consulted his iPad. Several keystrokes later, he announced, "The ocean temperature fluctuates between 77-86 degrees, year-round."

She sighed. "Between the museum project and the filming, I don't know if I can leave until spring. Or more likely summer."

Luc frowned. "If I can leave the restaurant for a while, you should be able to leave your work as well. That's why you have employees—to hold down the fort while you get away and recharge. And there's more to do there than just surfing. The country is a Garden of Eden. We can visit volcanoes and rain forests. And they have these crazy howler monkeys and neon-colored toucans. And coffee! The coffee is supposed to be out of this world!"

Luc looked so excited that Iris couldn't help but be swayed. "Okay," she said. "You may have sold me with the coffee part. But doesn't the camp have a one-week program? I don't know if I can get away for fourteen days."

"But we can't perfect our surfing if we only do the half-program."

"I can live with that. We can always go back next year to polish up our form." It did sound like this trip would be more than just baking on a beach. "They speak Spanish there, right? Mine is pretty rusty."

"My Spanish is decent, although after my years in Italy, I sometimes get it mixed up with Italian. I'm sure that a lot of people speak English, especially at the camp."

"I may be coming around. Just give me a little more time to think about it. Another day?"

Luc came up behind Iris, bent doen and kissed her neck. "It will be great for us. You know, they say travelling together is the real test of a relationship."

Do we need a test?

43

Even on a Sunday, this close to the election, Trent had to spend the day on stump speeches and pressing the flesh. He just finished giving yet another version of his help-the-homeless speech at a fundraising tea in Brookline. It was held at the estate of one of his big donors, and the spread was even bigger and more sumptuous than his own place in Weston. Deirdre was sizing up the architecture and the very expensive furnishings. He hoped that didn't signify another renovation, or God forbid, a move.

He turned to the next person in the receiving line with what he liked to think of as Mandela-like patience. A balding, middle-aged man with protruding eyes stuck out a hand. "Robert Buchanan from the *Globe*. Impressive speech, Congressperson Westbrook. I just have a quick question for you."

Trent glanced around for Edward, forgetting he'd sent him on a special assignment. "Press were not invited to this event," he said while signaling across the room with a raised finger to Tina Chung, his Chief of Staff.

"Does the property at 162 Highland Avenue in Somerville ring a bell for you? My sources tell me you're the owner behind the shell company known as 162 Highland Trust. Why the secrecy?"

The reporter's loud, grating voice carried, and a number of people nearby turned to stare. Tina arrived with two large men from Edward's security team. One of them dropped his hand to his belt, brushing his jacket open. The movement revealed, as it was intended to, the edge of a gun holster. They moved in on both sides of the reporter and smoothly escorted him out.

Trent put on an unsettling smile and shrugged. "Reporters, always trying to dig up a story where there isn't one," he said to the small crowd.

He felt the phone in his jacket pocket begin to vibrate an instant before the audible ring. "Excuse me," he said as he hurried outside to find a secluded spot in the garden.

"Edward. How did it go?"

"We now have leverage."

"Did anyone see you? Tell me you didn't use a puppy to lure the kid to your car."

"No one saw my men and best you don't know the details."

"Right. But he wasn't harmed?"

"No, sir."

"And you'll keep him in a secure place until this is over."

"Yes, sir."

Despite the cool October weather, Trent felt a bead of sweat trickle down the back of his neck, underneath his Charvet shirt and navy blazer. "You know I don't like to operate this way, but Jim's left me no choice."

44

Jim lounged on the main deck bench of this new woman's boat. He had met Amarette in Tootsie's Orchid Lounge in downtown Nashville on Saturday and spent an energetic night back at her condo. She had adorable freckles across her pert nose and the body of a woman much younger than her forty years. Jim was surprised when she'd invited him to spend Sunday on her fishing boat, an asset from her divorce. He figured, why not? She seemed lonely and since he needed to lie low anyway, he might as well enjoy it.

Amarette reeled in her fishing rod, looking disgusted. She'd had no luck all afternoon in catching a single bass in Lake Percy Priest, or was it catfish she was trying for? Jim, or Jamie as he was going by these days, pulled his trucker hat low to shield his eyes from the glare of the setting sun and admired the back view of her shapely legs in cut-off jeans. She pulled off the lure, tossed it into a compartment in the tackle box and replaced it with different bait.

"I don't understand this. I always catch at least one fish in this area."

"You gave it your best shot. Why don't we head in? There's that barbecue place near the marina. I'll buy you dinner."

Jim wasn't particularly into fishing, considered boats a waste of time with all the trouble and maintenance required, and was now finally growing bored after several hours studying Amarette's body from different angles as she fished. Besides, he was hungry.

"Let me try just one more spot," she said. "Then, I promise, we'll head back to the marina. Why don't you get yourself another beer?"

She climbed to the flying bridge and started the engine. It burbled powerfully as she maneuvered the boat farther down the edge of the lake, finally slowing to a stop in a small cove. They hadn't seen any other boats for the last hour, and it was getting dark. The mournful sound of a distant loon echoed off the murky water.

Amarette clambered back down to the teak-lined cockpit. "This is the best time to catch the suckers. This is when they feed." She gave him a wink and returned to the back of the boat to cast her line.

It was also when *he* usually fed, Jim thought irritably, and he was starting to get nervous about being in such an isolated place. As far as Jim could tell, he hadn't triggered any alarms which might have revealed his whereabouts to Trent. He paid for things in cash and resisted calling his son, although that temptation was growing stronger. He needed to stay hidden but realized that if Trent managed to locate him now, this would be a perfect spot to finish him off. Amarette couldn't be part of a plot, could she? Did she buy his act as Jamie Peterson from Providence?

Twenty minutes later, she lashed her rod and reel to the side of the boat. "I give up. No fish for us for dinner unless it's from a restaurant. We can head back now."

"Anything I can do to help?"

"No, you relax. We should be back at the dock and the restaurant in less than an hour, and you can have some of the best barbecue in the state." She mounted the ladder and Jim expected to hear the motor rev. But it didn't. He heard no sound. He went up to the flybridge to see if there was a problem. Amarette was checking gauges and switches. She looked up. "Damn thing won't start. It was working fine just before we stopped here."

"What's wrong?" he asked.

"We have gas, and I checked the emergency stop switch. Must be either an ignition problem or a bad electrical connection."

"Do you know how to check for that?"

"That was always my ex's department, but I can see if any wires look loose." She descended to the main deck and Jim peered down to see her lifting hatches and fiddling with things inside. He went to join her.

"Everything looks okay to me," she said. "That probably means a faulty ignition switch or something else we can't deal with here. Damn. We'll need to get back to the marina to have a mechanic look at it."

"How do we get back there if the engine won't start?"

Amarette led them up to the flybridge and fiddled with the knob on her marine radio. She said "Mayday" three times into the mouthpiece. "This is Spice Girl. We're stranded near Fall Creek Recreation Area on Lake Percy Priest near the shore. The engine won't start. I think it's an ignition issue. We need a tow back to the Nashville Shores Marina. Out."

They waited, listening to a crackling sound for several minutes. No one responded.

Amarette tried a second time. They waited and again, they heard static.

"Could we swim ashore and walk somewhere to get help?"

"We're in the middle of nowhere, honey."

Jim tried to keep himself from imagining that this was part of some plot involving Trent. He could picture himself in a watery grave with his son never knowing where he'd gone. He looked up. The moon was now overhead—a tiny, bright sliver, and the stars seemed to pop out of the sky.

Amarette gave the radio a third try, but this yielded the same result.

"Don't these emergency stations have to be monitored at all times?" Jim asked.

"I don't think our signal is going through." Amarette gave him an apologetic look. "Listen, there's a comfortable cabin down below and I can heat up some freeze-dried food that's not too bad. Why don't we make the best of it tonight? I'm sure other boats will be by in the morning, and they'll be able to help us."

Jim shrugged. He should go with the flow. "I suppose it could be worse. We still have plenty of beer."

Amarette looked at Jim coquettishly. "We should have a party in the stateroom. You don't have any place else to be tonight, do you?"

45

Trent couldn't believe that this was not working. He sat at his desk in campaign HQ and nervously checked the time on his Breitling. Ten-thirty on Monday morning, almost twenty hours after the kid was picked up.

He'd learned the details about the kidnapping on the news channels along with the rest of the public. Edward had used subcontractors to grab the kid while he was practicing shooting hoops against the garage backboard at his mother's house in Newton. The extraction was handled quickly, the only witness being a dogwalker who noted a gray Honda Accord at the reported time driving through the quiet neighborhood a little too fast. He hadn't gotten a license plate number or description of the driver.

The police issued an Amber Alert on Sunday afternoon and by 7 o'clock, the mother's heartbreaking appeal had been broadcast on all the TV stations and internet outlets. A school photo of the cherubic, gap-toothed seven-year-old had been splashed across the front pages of every newspaper in the country. And Trent had checked to be sure of that far-reaching coverage. So why wasn't his phone ringing?

This morning had seen another media blitz about the kid. An

unnamed source had leaked that there had been no blackmail demand yet, information had every parent in the country fearing the worst.

Trent and Deirdra had no children of their own. He pushed that thought back into the far recess of his mind where it resided. But Jimbo had seemed quite attached to this kid. Was his old classmate so far off the grid that he wasn't keeping up with the news? Maybe he'd slipped through Edward's dragnet and was sitting on a beach in New Caledonia with some nubile young thing, sipping some friggin' umbrella drink.

And if so, what was Trent supposed to do with the guy's kid?

46

Iris swung into her office on Monday morning to find Loretta at the reception desk, peering at something on her desktop screen.

"It's so sad," Loretta said, "the poor little kid who got kidnapped from his mom's backyard."

"What? When did that happen?"

"Yesterday afternoon. Look at this photo from the *Globe* article. Doesn't it just melt your heart?"

Iris circled the desk so she could see over Loretta's shoulder. A sweet-looking boy with floppy hair and a shy grin appeared on the screen. His name was Jimmy Dugan.

"Kidnapped, you said? How can people be that sick?"

"The mother made an appeal on the news last night and I almost cried."

"That's why I don't watch the TV news. It's too upsetting. Do the police have any leads?"

Loretta pressed her lips together. "They've identified a person of interest—the divorced father. But he seems to have disappeared."

"Well, I guess it's better if *he* has Jimmy than if a stranger's taken him. But hard on the mother, and probably traumatic for the kid, too."

"A reporter interviewed the mother, and she doesn't believe it was her ex. He wrote her a week ago to say he had to go out of town, but to tell their son he loved him."

Iris shook her head. "There's so much misery going around right now."

Loretta looked up from the monitor. "You went to Carl's memorial service? How is Milo holding up?"

"Not well. I'll see him this afternoon when we film the staircase unveiling."

Sheba let out a loud huff and flopped down on the floor at Iris's feet, glaring up at them—Sheba-speak for *stop yapping*.

"It's good that Milo has a big project like this to focus on," Loretta said.

"But Carl having been attacked right there in the building must be a constant reminder for him."

"Social media's taken to calling it the Museum of Horrors."

"Oh, damn. I told Alex I'd get Nili to try to counter some of that negative social media. I'd better do that now."

Iris and Sheba walked through the open office, stopping briefly at Rollo's desk to look at his design development drawings for Berkeley Street. Once back in her office, she called Nili to see what he could do about Twitter. He promised to have an intern work on it to satisfy Alex, but said he personally thought the attention would draw people to the new film and the museum. Iris confirmed that she would be ready for the make-up chair at noon, then rang off.

She spent the next half hour typing her notes for the afternoon film segment and practicing her lines. Nili would have his own ideas, but she'd resist his attempt to make her sound like some reality real estate make-over host.

As she was deciding what to order for an early lunch, her phone rang. She checked the caller ID, surprised her friend was calling back so soon.

"Hi, Alise. How are you?"

"Oh, Iris! Have you been following the kidnapping of that little boy?"

"It's terrible, isn't it?"

"But the name. It jogged my memory. The boy's name is Jimmy Dugan. Jimmy Jr."

"Uh, okay."

"And Jim Dugan, his father, was a student of mine about twenty years ago. I remember him. A big guy who was on the wrestling team."

Iris would have to find out more about him. If Jim Dugan had actually kidnapped his own son in a custody battle, maybe, as a teenager, he was capable of killing a homeless boy.

"I took out a few yearbooks from the school library this morning to check on when Jim Dugan went to G&B. He graduated in '04."

Iris thought for a minute. "And now the media is saying he has disappeared." Interesting timing, but she shouldn't jump to conclusions. Perhaps someone killed both Jim Jr. and Sr. for an unrelated reason. She hoped not.

"Why don't I drop these yearbooks by your office, and you can go through them. See if there's anything helpful in them."

"Thank you, Alise. That would be great."

Iris's pulse sped up. *Could all three of these crimes be connected?*

47

Iris took a bottle of cold brew coffee from the kitchenette fridge and poured it into a glass over ice. She carried it back to her office with the three school yearbooks that Alise had dropped off with Loretta.

The Class of 2004 volume was on top of the pile. She flipped open its thick pages to the senior portraits in the front. Jim Dugan's picture, unlike his son's, looked unremarkable. He had close-set eyes, short brown hair, and a bovine expression. Under his picture was the following background information: James Andrew Dugan /Jimbo/Wrestling Varsity 10,11,12/Baseball 9/Golf 11,12. The quote he had chosen was "Life is like a rollercoaster. Just when you think you're on top, you go flying back down and someone pukes on you."

Iris read the blurbs provided by the yearbook staff in an attempt to fill out the personality of each Senior. Jimbo's section was pathetically short: *Great golfer! Kegs' twin, Helped the wrestling team reach the semi-finals, one of the class giants.*

Iris had known "Jimbos" like him in her life. She doubted he was any kind of mastermind who could have kept a murder undetected for two decades. On the other hand, she could see him trailing behind someone else, an alpha dog, doing their bidding. And wasn't there was usually a second henchman as well, following dutifully behind the leader?

Was Kegs Jim's actual twin? She scanned the pages but didn't see another senior with the same last name. Maybe they were called twins because they hung out together.

Recalling her own regrettable high school years, Iris knew that someone in the class usually had an older brother or some other resource who could be bribed into buying beer for parties. This availability might have earned this friend-of-Jim the nickname. Iris thought back to all the stupid nicknames of people in her high school and college classes. The boy's name might actually start with a "K", like Kevin or Kirk. Maybe he was on the wrestling team with Jim. Sports so often forged strong bonds between teammates.

Iris flipped through the yearbook to the club and team photos further back, before the paid advertisements. She located the Wrestling team's pages and found a group shot showing Jim as several inches taller than the other heavily muscled boys. He must have been around six foot six, a giant wrestler. How did he manage to disappear recently with a physique like that?

The team in the photo was wearing those one-piece leotard-like uniforms, sleeveless and cut off above the knee. They looked like bathing suits from the 1920s. Iris read off the names of the teammates, matching them by row. There was a Kevin Linkletter, standing next to Jim. Kevin was a short wiry guy with a feeble attempt at a mustache.

Iris went back to the senior photos and found Kevin's page. No academic honors or class officer positions for him, either. His quote, "When's this due?" sounded like he and Jim might have shared an "I'm too cool for this" outlook on life. Scanning through the comments at the bottom of Kevin's page, Iris noted the words: *member of the trio*. Did that mean what she wanted it to mean? Was

Kevin Linkletter "Kegs"? Who was the third member of the group, their leader?

She skipped back to the wrestling team page and studied the photograph of the twelve boys. In the middle of the group stood one with a weak chin and a shrewd expression. He was by no means the strongest looking team member, but there was something magnetic about him. He looked like the type of kid who used strategy and ruthlessness rather than brawn to win his matches. She checked the caption for his name: Trent Westbrook. And he was the team captain. It figured. If he was the alpha, it would make sense that the betas, Jim and Kevin, would defer to their wrestling captain.

Trent Westbrook's name rang a bell for Iris. She googled him and found that he had become a congressman and was now running for the Senate. Uh, oh. This guy was high up on the food chain.

She'd see if Alise remembered these three students hanging around together. If so, Iris would pass along everything she'd learned and suspected to Lieutenant Garcia. But he would have to be on firmer ground than this before pursuing any accusations against a guy like Westbrook.

Iris decided to see where Kevin Linkletter was these days. An online search brought up an obituary mentioning his death several years before in a sailing accident on the North Shore of Massachusetts. And now Jim Dugan was missing. Interesting. If these three were the ones responsible for Sam Parker's death, then Ben Franklin's adage might apply: *Three may keep a secret if two are dead.*

48

On Monday morning, Jim used Amarette's binoculars to scan the horizon for approaching boats. She was up on the flybridge, trying again to rouse someone on the radio. The sun had risen several hours before, but the only sounds were a dawn chorus of birdcalls, the static hum of insect wings, and the lapping of waves against the shoreline rocks. It was incredibly peaceful. He tried to separate out the chirping of robins from the songs of warblers and sparrows. A month ago, he'd been helping Jimmy prepare for his birding badge test in Cub Scouts.

Jim leaned back against a cushion and closed his eyes. He'd hear any outboard motors that came close. It was relaxing being so far off the grid, the boat rocking gently. It felt like being in a protective bubble.

He awoke to the dark silhouette of Amarette standing in front of a blaze of sunlight, holding out another cup of god-awful instant coffee. "Looks like my scout is asleep at the wheel. Did I tire you out last night?"

Jim rubbed his eyes and set the coffee cup down on a side table. "Sorry, did I miss anything? Is the radio working?"

"Still no reception. But there should be some fishing boats coming by soon. I'll try casting my line again while we're waiting. How does a grilled smallmouth bass sound for lunch?"

"You catch it, I'll eat it."

Jim regretted that offer as soon as he took his first bite of catfish. He'd had misgivings as she cleaned the ugly creatures and he saw how much dirt was inside. But the muddy, fishy taste was beyond awful. He tried valiantly to keep chewing. Smiling and chewing. "Interesting taste. Please pass the chips."

Jim cut the fish into little pieces and tried to will his plate to appear empty. He kept washing tiny pieces down with large sips of beer. But just as he was about to confess his dislike of catfish to Amarette, he heard the sound of rescue: a motor put putting in the distance. Jim grabbed the binoculars and rushed to the side of the cockpit to see a dark speck heading their way.

"Shucks. We're having such fun out here." Amarette sighed. "Now we'll have to go back to civilization."

"All good things must come to an end," Jim fibbed. He took their plates into the galley.

Ten minutes later, a small pontoon boat approached, a white-haired couple its sole occupants.

Jim and Amarette waved their arms. The boat pulled alongside the Spice Girl.

"You folks having engine trouble?" The man's face looked painfully pink from sunburn.

Amarette nodded. "I think we need a new ignition switch, or it might be a different electrical problem. We've been stranded since last night. Our radio and cell phones don't get any reception here."

"Oh, dear. Let's see if ours work, Frank," the woman said. "Maybe we can get through on Channel 16 to the Army Corps."

Jim spent the next few minutes barely breathing as he worried about an Army Corps officer identifying him, but Frank's efforts on his radio and both cell phones yielded the same result as Amarette's. "Must be a dead zone. Where do you need to get to?"

"I keep the boat at the Nashville Shores Marina." Amarette said. "They have mechanics there who can figure out the problem and fix it."

Frank looked at their larger, heavier Spice Girl doubtfully. "We rented this pontoon boat for the morning to take a little pleasure ride. We're headed back to the Elm Hill Marina now. If you want to hop aboard, we can drop you at your marina and you can send someone out here to tow the boat. I don't think this boat's engine is strong enough to do the job."

Amarette and Jim accepted the offer of a lift. They locked up Spice Girl's cabin, checked that the anchor was secure, and climbed aboard the pontoon boat for the agonizingly slow trip back to Nashville Shores. By the end of the hour, they knew all about Frank and Marge's sulky teenage granddaughter and ungrateful college-age grandson.

Back at their own marina, Amarette headed toward the maintenance office. Jim pointed to the barbecue restaurant on the far side of the parking lot.

"I'll get us a snack for the ride back to town, okay?"

49

Iris arrived on foot at the Museum project at 11:30. She carried a glass jar containing a thick maroon smoothie of beets and kale for her lunch on-the-go. Milo and Dewey were standing in the atrium, studying the giant wooden frame of the curved staircase.

Milo turned as she approached. "I hope the film guys aren't expecting to see a finished staircase today."

"No," Iris said. "I explained to Nili that it would be a rough frame at this point. That all the finished surfaces would get installed at the end." She stood back to observe the volume of the stairs against the tall opening of the central space with its extending balconies. "It looks great. I think the proportions are perfect."

Milo looked past her. "Your design. I sent the rest of the crew home since we can't make any noise while you're filming. This will delay the schedule."

His manner was uncharacteristically chilly. Was he mad at her? Filming the construction wasn't her idea. "I heard your band playing at *the Plough* on Saturday. You guys are awesome."

"I saw you. You didn't stay long."

"It was packed. You've got quite a following."

The beeping of the new alarm system interrupted them as the front door opened and Nili punched in the security code. The grip noisily rolled the camera rig into the atrium, his belt studded with clothespins. A young woman in black glasses, jeans and a blazer followed Nili, rolling in a compact equipment box of her own.

"Iris, this is Lauren Davenport," Nili said. Lauren reached out to shake Iris's hand. "She hosts the Podcast *Beantown Life* and is here to interview you. Her show airs at one o'clock, so she'd like to record you after you finish our segment for the film."

Iris was about to protest when Nili held up a hand. "Alex Harcon already okayed it. This is about dealing with the Twitter crap about the project."

"It's just a five-minute spot," Lauren said. "Don't worry. We keep everything loose, and it will be good publicity for the museum. We're all on the same side here."

"I'd like to see your questions beforehand." Iris said.

"That's not how we work," Lauren responded. "It's live, spontaneous, real. We don't want any canned answers."

Iris looked over at Nili, and he shrugged. "You asked me to address the Twitter comments. This is the best way to do that. Lauren has a huge following."

Tonya beckoned Iris over to her makeshift hair and make-up table in a corner of the room. "Time to apply the magic for the camera, hon."

Iris took a chair in front of Tonya while the older woman applied a veil of hairspray. She read over her prepared notes for the film segment and sipped her smoothie. Recording a podcast made her nervous. She wasn't good at thinking on her feet and worried she'd blurt out the wrong thing. Doing this was definitely not part of her contract for the film or for her architectural work.

Tonya added a coat of eyeliner and some red lipstick to Iris's everyday make-up, finishing up with a dusting of powder. Iris turned over the chair to Milo.

"Why do men get the best eyelashes?" Tonya mused. She brushed some powder on his face, and he stood up.

Iris suggested to him that they go over their segment together. "I'd like to start with some general comments about why I designed different size rooms for the different scale artworks instead of leaving the space as a big open box. Now that you've put up the metal studs for the side galleries, maybe we can walk through the new rooms, then end up in the atrium, talking about the staircase. Is there anything you want to mention?"

"No, I'm good trailing mutely behind you."

Iris looked carefully at him. "What's up, Milo? Have I done something wrong? You seem really pissed at me."

"I'm sorry. I shouldn't take it out on you."

"Obviously, you're very upset about Carl. Is that it? But I want to know if you are angry at me."

"I just want to get my hands on the bastard who killed him."

"So do I!"

Milo relaxed a bit. "Have you heard anything more from Garcia?"

Iris tried to remember what the Police Lieutenant had actually confirmed and what was just part of her theory. Before she could answer Milo, the sound person slipped in and clipped on their mics. Nili directed them to their opening marks taped on the floor.

She and Milo moved through the sequence of the new museum spaces, Nili following with the stabilized moving camera. Iris was feeling the too-few hours of sleep she'd had the night before and tried consciously to animate her speech. Milo offered a few relevant comments, seeming to emerge from his funk. They ended at the new staircase with Iris and Milo discussing the intent of the design and construction details.

By the time Nili called "cut" Iris was tired but noticed Lauren fiddling with recording equipment over at Tonya's former workstation. She wished she could cancel this whole podcast session and go home.

Lauren, wearing a large pair of headphones, sat in front of a large, flat box with sliding levers and dials. Two microphones were positioned on stands. Lauren gestured to the seat across from her and pointed to the second set of headphones. Showtime again, this time live on-air.

Iris watched the countdown of a digital clock on the table. 4-3-2-1…

"This is Lauren Davenport, your host for another session of *Beantown Life*. My guest today is the very talented Iris Reid, the architect for the Alex Harcon Museum in Cambridge you've been hearing so much about lately." Lauren's voice had shifted into a purr, almost a caress of her unseen audience. "We're here on the construction site that Ms. Reid is transforming into a stunning new building with a breathtaking central atrium and a curving staircase. But the architecture, however wonderful, is not what everyone's talking about. It's the fact that two people have died in the space where we're sitting now, one twenty years ago and one just last week. What can you tell us about those tragedies, Ms. Reid? Do you feel the presence of their ghosts?"

Oh, shit. Iris glared at Nili. "Well, Lauren, we're very sad about our carpenter's recent death, and feel bad for the young man who was killed twenty years ago. But let me correct some of your facts. We don't know where the boy was actually killed. His skeletal remains were hidden in the building at some point, and recently removed by the Cambridge police. Our head carpenter, Carl Nowak, was attacked here last week and later died in the hospital. We think he was assaulted by someone trying to dig up those bones from the past."

Lauren wore the trace of a smile. "And do you know if the police have any leads to the identity of the recent attacker?"

"I wouldn't know."

"But weren't you there when the boy's remains were discovered? And I heard from my source that you might have identified a clue the murderer left behind in the floorboards. Is that true?"

Where was this woman getting her information? From the film crew who saw me studying the blue cloth? "There may be a person of interest who the police are trying to locate."

"And your clue led to this suspect! Exciting! How are the police trying to find him?"

"His picture was in today's..." Iris's voice trailed off. *What have I just said?*

A quick, feral intelligence showed in Lauren's glittering eyes. She cocked her head. "The prominent picture of a missing male in today's papers is of James Dugan. Is that who you mean? Is he a person of interest in the attacks in this museum, *as well as* the recent kidnapping of his son?"

Iris's eyes widened. "That's not what I said. And Carl died in a hospital," she finished lamely. She took off her headphones, rose to her feet, and stalked away from the table. She could hear Lauren delivering her windup of the podcast.

"Well, you've heard it here first, folks. James Dugan may just be the Museum of Horror killer, at least according to Iris Reid, the museum's architect. We sincerely hope that Little Jimmy Junior remains safe, wherever he may be."

50

Milo ran out behind Iris to the sidewalk outside the museum. "What the hell? The cops have a suspect and you didn't tell me?"

Nili's head popped out of the doorway, and as he was opening his mouth to say something, Iris shouted, "Not now!" She grabbed Milo's arm. "Let's get out of here."

She looked around, then pointed left. "The Chinese restaurant. Quick—before the vampire podcaster can extract any more blood."

The tiny restaurant was half a block away and they reached the door before anyone else came after them. They climbed up to the second-floor dining room and found an empty table in the back.

Iris glanced around at the tiki bar decor. "I've never been here before, have you?"

"No," Milo responded. "And don't try to change the subject."

Iris groaned. "Did I really say on a live podcast that Jim Dugan was a suspect in the museum killings? Garcia is going to kill me."

"You sort of did. *Is* he a suspect?" Milo asked.

They stopped talking long enough to read the menu and order

virgin Mai Tais from the server. "And some pork dumplings." Iris added. "Stress makes me hungry."

Iris started to chew on her thumbnail, then stopped herself. "I've been piecing together some things myself, trying to find the assailant. This morning I found some information that led me to Jim Dugan. I haven't even spoken about it to Lieutenant Garcia, and you and I haven't had a chance to really talk. I can't believe I blurted it out on the podcast. I hope Lauren Davenport doesn't have many listeners."

"Supposedly, five thousand. So, now tell me…every goddamned thing."

Iris nervously shredded her paper napkin as she filled him in on the trail she'd been following, the one that seemed to lead to Jim Dugan.

When she finished talking, Milo waggled his head skeptically. "I can go with the killers being some students from that school, but why pick out Dugan because he was there then and is in the news now? That's a stretch. There might have been countless trios of thugs there then. And the idea that Trent Westbrook was the ringleader? It could well be true, but you're really playing with fire, coming to that conclusion. He'd probably sue your ass off if you damaged his run for the Senate."

"Since I didn't mention Westbrook on air, it'll only be Jim Dugan who sues my ass off." Iris chewed on a dumpling. "But wait. The other kid who was good friends with Dugan at school died in a boating accident a few years ago."

Milo took the umbrella out of his cocktail and ate the cherry speared on its end. "It happens. A kid in his orbit came to a bad end."

"And now Dugan's missing. What if Westbrook killed the homeless boy twenty years ago and Dugan and his friend were witnesses. Now, Westbrook needs to eliminate anyone who has dirt on him."

Milo gave her a wry smile. "I'd like to say that a politician running for the Senate would be more ethical than that, but we both know that's not true."

Her phone started chiming with incoming calls. Harcon, Nili, Garcia and Robert "Budge" Buchanan, the *Boston Globe* reporter who was her nemesis back in college. She silenced it. Instead, she punched in Alise's number.

"Hi Alise."

"Were the yearbooks any help?"

"I think so. It looks like Jim Dugan was friends with a student nicknamed 'Kegs.' Does that ring a bell?"

"Was he a short boy? I remember he had a sidekick and the two of them looked like Mutt and Jeff."

"He looks short standing next to Jim in the wrestling team photo. I think his real name was Kevin something."

"Hmm. That does sound familiar."

"Any chance those two hung out with Trent Westbrook?"

"Oh, that's right, the politician. He was in that class too. I think he was also a wrestler and in the student government. I do think those three always hung out together. Trent Westbrook has become a big donor to the school. I can't imagine him mixed up in anything like this."

Iris ended the call, then noticed a new text message from Budge:

> Hey Reid, I'll tell you my information if you tell me yours. CALL ME!

51

The aroma alone inside the barbecue restaurant sent Jim into a state of bliss. He studied the take-out menu on the plastic sign over the counter. Pulled-pork, baby-back ribs, or brisket? Why not all three?

He was the only one in line in the nearly deserted place and it took several fake coughs to get the attention of the teenager at the grill. "Can I get a combo plate with extra cole slaw please?"

"Hush puppies with that?" the kid drawled. "Cokes?"

"It comes with corn bread, right? No hush puppies. One iced tea and one coffee." He set down two crisp twenties next to the cash register.

Jim leaned against the counter while he waited for his order to be assembled. The darkness inside the room contrasted with rectangles of bright sunlight entering through the small, curtained windows. Lunchtime was over, and a dozen tables with checked tablecloths were set up for the dinner crowd.

Jim felt relieved to be back in civilization, although he couldn't say why. Wasn't the point of being in hiding to be away from anyone who might report his presence to Trent, or to the cops if they were looking for him? And he'd had a lot of fun with Amarette this weekend. He hadn't met any women at home who were as easy-going as she. If it wasn't for Jimmy being in the Boston area (and he knew his ex would never move), Jim might consider relocating down here once the coast was clear.

But what would it take to make the coast clear? Would Trent let the Harvard Square botch-up slide once he was securely placed in the Senate? The election was less than two weeks away. As far as Jim knew, the cops hadn't identified him as the lumberjack's assailant. But he hadn't been able to check the news in two days. Jim saw a basket near the door overflowing with newspapers people left behind on their way out. Maybe he could grab a few and find some mention of the case. He headed in that direction.

"Your order's ready," the teenager called out.

Jim turned around and returned to the counter. He tossed some plastic utensils into the bags and was adding sugar and cream to his coffee when he felt a hand around his waist. "Everything's all set with the boat," Amarette said. "What's all this? Are you still hungry?" She picked up the drinks and several napkins. Jim collected the two laden bags and followed her.

"We can drive back to my place in town and have ourselves a picnic out on the deck," Amarette said.

Jim's good mood faded fast. As they left the restaurant, all he could focus on was how much he wanted a taste of that barbecue *right now.*

52

Trent viewed his plate of bratwurst and sauerkraut warily. He'd just come from the Rusty Nail Diner in Dedham where he'd drunk too much weak coffee and consumed several jelly doughnuts at a candidate's Q and A sponsored by the *Dedham Eagle*. His stomach was roiling. Now, at 1:30, this was a late lunch at the Golden Farms Orchard, currently celebrating Octoberfest. At this rate, he would have to have his custom suits let out.

Locals crowded around the picnic table to ask questions and take selfies with him. Trent's mouth was aching from smiling. He answered the usual inquiries about his position on abortion, taxes, and climate change initiatives, parroting his speechwriters' carefully crafted responses. These people always asked the same things. Why couldn't they just read his position papers?

Tina Chung, his Chief of Staff, leaned over and whispered in his ear, "Chat up the woman in the blue pantsuit at the other end of the table. She's the head of Whitmill College."

Trent was fake-smiling his way through the crowd when his burner phone vibrated in his jacket's inner pocket. He raised it to his ear. "Can't really talk now, Edward," he grinned.

"It's important, sir. Can you meet me in the parking lot? I'm in my car. We need to speak privately."

Trent asked Tina where the restrooms were and headed off in that general direction, veering off toward the parking lot when he was out of view of the gathering. It took a minute for him to pick out Edward's black SUV from all the other similar ones, but he soon slipped into the passenger seat and turned to his head of security. "What's happened?"

"Dugan's been tentatively identified by the museum's architect as the killer on the Harvard Square construction site and also responsible for the twenty-year-old murder."

"What? By the *architect*? Did the police put out a press release? I don't understand."

Edward placed a finger on each temple and made tiny circles. "It happened on a podcast called *Beantown Life*. The architect was being questioned about the project being called 'the Museum of Horror,' and she implied that Dugan was responsible for both murders in the building. It seemed like a slip, but the media picked up on it. It's gone viral on Twitter. The police are keeping mum about their position."

"How did she make the connection?"

"I have no idea."

"We need to find out what she knows and how she found it out. If both murders are pinned on Dugan and Dugan disappears permanently, our problem is solved. But if this architect knows that there were other people involved in the first killing, and they tie Dugan to me from our high school association…"

"Do you want me to pick her up, sir?"

"We can't make the situation worse. Let me think." After a minute, Trent brightened. "Remember our debrief session with Kegs before his sailing accident?"

"I do."

"Would something like that work?"

Edward tipped his head. "I believe it might, but I'll have to act fast."

53

After Iris ended her call with Alex Harcon, she looked over at Milo.

"Sorry. I need to put these fires out." Iris hoped she'd managed to dig herself out of the podcast mess convincingly with Alex. The one text she avoided answering was from "Budge" Buchanan, the *Globe* reporter. They sometimes put aside their college antagonism and swapped useful information, but Iris wanted to be on a firmer footing about Dugan before she chanced another media blunder.

Milo laid some bills down on the table and stood. "As much as I'm enjoying watching you try to do damage control, some of us are on a deadline."

"Are you going back to the museum? I'll walk with you on the way back to my office."

Five minutes later, after Milo disappeared into the building, Iris turned toward Brattle Street and spotted Budge himself moving toward her at a fast clip. He was staring at his phone and didn't see her. She pivoted around to avoid him, heading east on Mount Auburn Street, when a black SUV with tinted windows pulled up alongside her. The rear door opened and a man in a black jacket with a baclava over his face reached out and grabbed her arm. Iris twisted away from him and called out to Budge. She caught his eye, but it was too late. The man in the baclava muscled her into the back seat, and the car sped away.

Iris tried to wriggle out of the man's grip, but he wrapped an arm around her neck. She raked her fingers across his cheek, digging into the flesh.

"Bitch!" he yelled.

The pressure on her throat let up. Iris turned toward the door and reached for the handle. But before she could turn it, she felt a damp rag held tightly over her mouth and nose, with an awful chemical smell. As she slipped out of consciousness, she wondered if her kidnapper was Jim Dugan, out for payback for her accusation.

54

Trent and Edward jogged along the leafy suburban streets of Weston. There were no sidewalks outside of the small town center, so they had to periodically dodge enormous SUVs passing erratically, with their drivers seemingly attending to their smartphones and video displays.

"She got all this... from scrap of material... left behind with... homeless kid?" Trent was feeling winded, but noticed with irritation that Edward was breathing easily, barely breaking a sweat.

"Apparently, she recognized the distinctive blue of your private school, sir. Architects have high color sensitivity, I'm told."

"And math teacher recognized... Dugan in the news... and put together... he went to G&B twenty years ago... How hell... that incriminate him?"

"You're missing the point, sir. It's not about whether Ms. Reid's assumptions are correct. It's about whether she *believes* they are correct. She has the visibility to draw attention to Dugan. If the police start digging into him as a suspect, they might be able to trace his movements on the night the carpenter got assaulted."

They stopped for a break and Trent considered this as he took a swig from his water bottle. "Did she mention me?"

"Yes, sir. She saw a wrestling team picture and some remarks under your senior yearbook photo and deduced that you, Kegs, and Dugan were high school friends. She'd been told that there were three boys that grabbed Sam Parker that night and thought that it might have been you."

"God's sake. Where's this woman getting information?"

"Evidently, the architect made contact with Sam Parker's girlfriend from back then. Ms. Reid said she couldn't remember the woman's name."

"Friggin' nightmare! Who's she told this story to?"

"Unfortunately, she's laid out her theory to Lieutenant Garcia, but she didn't think he believed her. She also talked to the old G&B math teacher, her contractor, and Alex Harcon."

They jogged into a small park, and Trent stopped at a bench, taking several deep breaths. He checked his heart rate on his Apple watch's fitness tracker. "Harcon? Shit. That guy's got the funds to hire a P.I. if he wants to get these murders solved and clear the stain from his museum. So, what do we do now?"

Edward continued jogging in place. "The easiest solution is to eliminate Dugan and pin everything on him, start to finish. But we haven't managed to flush him out yet."

"Can't believe he hasn't responded. What's happening with the kid? He's still okay?"

"Yes, sir. We've given him a Game Boy and some books to keep him occupied."

"What's a Game Boy?'

"An old school computer game console. Point is, he can't use it to contact anyone. We have this under control."

"What do we do with him if Jimbo never surfaces?"

Edward looked blank. "We can't set the boy loose. He's seen too much."

Trent stared down at his shoes. "Right. And what about the

architect? Why is she investigating this? So far, Nancy Drew here seems way too clever in putting the pieces together. At some point, Garcia may start listening to her."

"All her so-called evidence is speculation. And no one saw us pick her up or drop her off today, so there's no proof that anything happened. She won't remember a thing. You didn't want us to pile up any more bodies than necessary, remember?"

"I'm starting to regret my caution. Let's keep an eye on her. She may become necessary collateral damage."

55

The takeout barbecue had cooled down by the time Jim and Amarette settled out on the deck of her condo for dinner, but Jim wolfed it down with relish. They watched the flaming pink and bruised violet of the sunset reflected in the glass of the downtown AT&T tower, known locally as the "Batman" building.

"My, Jamie, you act like you haven't eaten in days. Haven't I been feeding you enough?"

In his persona as Jamie Peterson, with a new trimmed beard, longer hair, and a tan, he no longer resembled any photos the police might be circulating if they'd connected him to the fatal attack on the lumberjack. Trent would probably try to track him down by way of his digital footprint but, so far, Jim had managed to stay off the grid. Still, he desperately wanted to speak with his son. Could Trent trace a call from a new burner phone?

Amarette's voice interrupted his thoughts. "Do you play golf, Sugar?"

He studied her face. Had he slipped and told her anything about his former life? "I've been known to play. How about you?"

Her smile made her look feline. "I'm an excellent golfer. We should play together. I'm a member at the Richland Country Club which has a sweet 18-hole course nearby. I'll call tomorrow and see if they have any open spots. Tuesdays during work hours are usually slow."

Jim panicked. Would he run into anyone he knew? The golf world could get pretty incestuous sometimes. "I don't have my clubs with me."

Amarette waved her hand. "Easy enough to rent." She gave him an appraising look. "I'll bet you're good. You certainly are, er, athletic."

Jim smiled sheepishly. At this point, he needed a night to himself. And maybe he should back away from this relationship. Amarette had too much spare time on her hands, with no need to work thanks to the generous proceeds from her divorce. He couldn't risk getting too close to anyone.

Amarette stood up to carry their dinner dishes back to the kitchen, and Jim rose to help her. She nodded toward the large TV in the family room. "Why don't you turn on the national news? I wonder if anything important's happened in the world while we've been away."

Jim set the glasses and crumpled napkins on the counter, then circled back to pick up the television remote control from the adjoining room. He turned on the TV and watched as the NewsChannel5 logo appeared on the screen. He dropped heavily onto the sofa and followed the opening stories about an assortment of wars in foreign lands and continued political dysfunction closer to home. Amarette came in from the kitchen and joined him on the sofa. "Guess we didn't miss much."

But just then, Jimmy Jr.'s second grade school photo filled the screen, his expression a sweet smile. The announcer's grim voice stated, "The search for Little Jimmy Dugan continues into its second day."

Jim let out a sharp breath. "NO!" he shouted.

Amarette looked alarmed. "What is it, Jamie? You look like you've seen a ghost."

Jim held up a hand for quiet so he could hear the story.

The newscaster continued, "As we reported earlier, Jimmy was kidnapped from the backyard of his mother's house in Newton, Massachusetts on Sunday afternoon. No word has been received from the presumed kidnappers. His father, James Dugan, Senior, is considered a person-of-interest in this case."

An unflattering photo of Jim from The Country Club flashed up on the screen. Amarette didn't seem to recognize his former self.

"If anyone has seen this seven-year-old boy or his father, please notify the phone number listed below." A chyron across the bottom of the screen scrolled the hot line number.

Jim grabbed a pen and a scrap of paper from the coffee table to write it down.

"Jamie—do you know anything about this boy or the father?" Amarette asked. "You need to tell the police. Think of that poor mother!"

Jim stood up, shaking. "I think I might. I'm going back to my place, and I'll call them from there." He gave her a quick kiss, grabbed his jacket, and ran out the door.

56

Iris awoke, propped up on a pillow in a hospital bed. Her throat felt sore, her head ached, and she was nauseous. *How had she gotten here?*

A uniformed police officer sat in a chair by the door, watching her. "Ms. Reid, I'm Officer John Slater from the Cambridge Police Department. I need to ask you some questions. Do you feel up to that?"

"What am I doing here?" The clock on the wall read 6:05. Hadn't she left the restaurant well before 2? What the hell happened during that missing time? Was it even the same day? She looked down at the hospital gown she was wearing. "Where are my clothes?"

"They're in the closet with your purse and phone. It doesn't appear that you've been robbed. Someone found you lying on the bank of the Charles River under a bridge and called 9-1-1. An ambulance brought you here to Mount Auburn Hospital to be checked out."

It crossed her mind that this was where Carl Nowak had died. She banished that thought and tried to take an assessment of possible injuries. Nothing major hurt. Had she been assaulted, or God forbid, raped?

A tall woman in a white coat knocked on the doorjamb and entered, smiling kindly at Iris. "Good, you're awake. I'm Doctor Harris. It seems like you've had quite an afternoon. We've run a battery of tests, and everything checks out. No sign of injury or assault, thank heavens. But your bloodwork shows trace amounts of chloroform and sodium pentothal. The latter is a rapid-onset short-acting barbiturate. Do you remember what was happening before you lost consciousness?"

"The last thing I recall is dumplings in a Chinese restaurant with my contractor, Milo. I think we walked back to the building we're renovating on Mount Auburn Street. I'm an architect."

The policeman moved closer. And held up his phone. "I need to get a full name and contact information for Milo as well as the name of that restaurant."

"Sure, but he would never drug me."

The doctor rested a hand on Iris's shoulder. "I'll let you speak with this officer. You're free to check out after you meet with the nurse in discharge. Take it easy for the rest of the day and drink lots of water until the drugs are fully out of your system. That may take a few more hours. You shouldn't have any residual problems." She headed out of the room.

Iris got up and retrieved her possessions from the closet. She was giving Milo's information to Officer Slater just as Luc rushed in, followed by a serious-looking man with tennis-ball fuzz on his head.

"Thank God. Are you okay?" Luc wrapped her in his arms, then leaned back and studied her face. "Budge said you'd been abducted! I was waiting at home with this FBI agent to hear from the kidnappers, and the hospital called. What happened?"

"I'm not sure. I was with Milo, then everything went blank."

The agent spoke quietly to the policeman in the corner, after which point Officer Slater left the room.

Luc sat Iris down on the edge of the bed and took her hand.

"Milo said you walked back from a restaurant together and he went into the museum building. You were headed back to your office. Budge happened to be in the area and saw someone grab you from the sidewalk and pull you into a black SUV. Don't you remember?"

"Budge saw someone abduct me from the street? I don't remember any of this."

"I was afraid you were dead!" Luc gestured toward the agent. "This FBI agent is here to find out who took you."

The man with the fuzzy head stepped forward, hand outstretched. He had the face of a middle-aged Ken doll. She shook his hand.

"Ms. Reid. I'm Agent Gene Kramer from the FBI's Boston office. We were notified by Mr. Buchanan that he witnessed you being abducted from Mount Auburn Street at 2:03 this afternoon. He pursued the car, but it sped through the intersection and headed toward Central Square before he could catch up with it. Mr. Buchanan got the license plate, but it belongs to a stolen station wagon."

Agent Kramer dragged a chair over and sat next to her bed. "I'm heading up the investigation into the disappearance of Jimmy Dugan Junior. We understand you made some sort of accusation on a podcast this afternoon tying Jimmy's father to some murders which occurred in a museum building you're renovating. I need to find out what happened to you and if it's related to your accusation about Dugan."

Luc cleared his throat. "I'd like to be present for the interview. Iris has been through a lot today."

She gave him a wan smile.

Kramer nodded. "That's fine, as long as you keep what's discussed confidential." He lay his phone on the bedside table and pressed a button to start recording, identifying the people in the room and the time. "James Dugan Senior is a person of interest in my case. We need to locate him. Did you recognize the people who took you? Was it Dugan? I need you to tell me everything you recall."

Iris took a sip of water from the paper cup next to her. "You said they pulled me into a car? I wish I could remember. Why would these people kidnap me, then let me go? I mean, I'm glad they did, but what was the point?"

"Your abductors might have wanted to find out what made you connect Jim Dugan to the murders in your museum. We're interested in that information as well. The podcast has generated a lot of attention in the online world. They might have drugged you to get you to reveal anything you'd discovered and who you might have told about it. The drugs wear off after a few hours, but you won't remember much of anything that happened or where you'd been held. That's why they let you go."

Iris considered this and shook her head. "The doctor said I'd have no aftereffects, but now I'm worried.

Agent Kramer tilted his head. "Your doctor told me they used sodium pentothal, also known as 'truth serum.' It's sometimes used as an anesthetic, so it's reasonably safe. Be grateful they chose a nonlethal approach."

Iris and Luc exchanged a long, worried look. He kissed the top of her head.

Kramer continued, "Why don't you run me through the reasons you think Dugan was involved with the Sam Parker and Carl Nowak murders. Then I need to know who you've told about this. Those people may also be in danger. The FBI needs to be aware of everything that the kidnappers might now know."

What had she revealed? Had she put Milo and Alise in danger?

57

Trent switched off the late Monday night news in his home office. Every station was flogging the Little Jimmy kidnapping story for all it was worth. Deirdre was out in the family room, glued to one of her reality TV shows, so he had time to evaluate the situation. He knew that he'd taken a huge risk using the kid to lure out Dugan. In retrospect, it was too high visibility, with public sentiment now aroused and the FBI sniffing around. It never dawned on him that Jim wouldn't respond quickly.

The muffled trill of his burner phone rang from his jacket pocket. He answered it.

"Edward, tell me you have some good news. Have your contacts located Jim?"

"No, and the rest of the news is not good, sir. Jimmy Jr. has escaped."

"Wait... what? He's a seven-year-old kid. How did he escape from your goddamn security guards?"

"He crawled out a small window in the bathroom. My men thought he was taking a bath, so they gave the kid some privacy. The boy had been totally compliant up until then, so they dropped their guard. Believe me, heads will roll."

"Oh, for God's sake. This is not acceptable. Your bozos need to find the kid before he can tell anyone what he knows."

"Yes, sir. He won't get far. It's dark up in Maine now and the temperature is dropping into the 30s. Jimmy's wearing only a sweatshirt and jeans. He's in the middle of Baxter State Park, over 200,000 acres of wilderness. I doubt he'll make it through the night. But my men are searching with night vision goggles. In the morning, if he's still missing, they'll send up drones to look for him and search using ATVs."

"We can't leave his body out there for hikers to find."

"No, sir. We'll make sure to put him where no one will find him."

"And this can't get out. No leaks. If Dugan does surface, he has to think we still have his son. You recorded the video, right?"

"Yes, sir. He was holding today's newspaper, but we can doctor that."

Trent leaned back in his wing chair and thumbed his chin. "I suppose this resolves the issue of what to do with the kid. If Jimmy dies of hypothermia tonight, it's due to his own disobedience and an act of God."

58

Jim tried to think straight as he jogged the ten blocks back to his rental apartment. His heart felt like it was breaking. That bastard Trent had taken his precious son. Jimmy must be scared. He had to save him. More than a day had gone by already. What was the smart move? Was there a smart move? If it came to it, he was more than willing to exchange himself for Jimmy, but how could he be sure that, once Trent found out Jim's location, he wouldn't kill them both?

Jim entered the building and sprinted up the stairs. He slammed his apartment door shut, and sat down at the small kitchen table, opening his laptop and searching for any coverage of Jimmy's disappearance. He needed to put together a plan, pronto.

The Boston Globe's website had the most extensive coverage of the case, revealing that the FBI was now involved. Jim thought quickly—his ex-wife must be going crazy with worry. He was amazed that she cast doubt on the idea that he had abducted Jimmy. And there was a very curious revelation in the evening digital *Globe*. It reported that the architect for the Harvard Square building had implied on a podcast earlier that day that Jim might be a person-of-interest in the two murders that had taken place there. WTF???!! How had she come to that conclusion? Or had Trent fed her that information so he could pin everything on Jim before getting rid of him?

Whoa. Hadn't he seen a TV show with this situation? The little fish got immunity from the FBI for telling what he knew about the big fish while also pretending to turn himself over to the big fish in exchange for his girlfriend. Would that work for Jim? Once Jimmy was safe, the FBI could move in and arrest Trent. But would that somehow get Jimmy or both of them killed?

Even if he made a deal in return for information on Trent, he'd probably get a reduced sentence and end up spending some time in prison for one or both murders. He knew he deserved to be punished.

Jim still remembered that poor, skinny homeless boy and what they had done to him twenty years ago when they were in high school. The kid had made the mistake of lifting Trent's wallet when the jerk went to Harvard Square to score some weed. The next day at school, Trent took Kegs and Jim aside, saying that they were going back to the Square that night at midnight to retrieve his wallet and teach the thief a lesson.

Maybe things wouldn't have gone so wrong if Trent hadn't just bought a stun gun off the internet that he was itching to try out. They learned later that he'd stashed it, along with a framing hammer, in his backpack.

It didn't take long for Trent to spot the kid, even in the dark. He was lurking on the outskirts of the Pit, probably looking for another oblivious mark to rob. Trent came up quietly behind him, put him in a chokehold, and dragged him into the secluded entryway of a jewelry store. "Where's my wallet?" he'd hissed in the kid's ear.

"I don't have it," the kid had protested, trying to squirm away. "I took the cash and threw it out. I'll give you back the money, man. Just let me go."

"Guess we'll have to teach him a lesson, won't we, boys? You picked the wrong guy to hit, asshole."

Being on the wrestling team, Kegs and Jim were used to a certain amount of controlled violence. Trent was the team captain, and the other two were accustomed to taking orders from him. At least that's what Jim told himself to try to justify what they did next.

They dragged the kid over to a small building in the Square where Trent's father had a branch office for his accounting firm. Trent had the key to the front door from when he had interned there over the summer. He flicked on the lights, and they dragged the kid into this big open space on the first floor. In the light, the boy looked about sixteen. He was short and cave-chested, looking like he hadn't eaten a decent meal in a long time. Jim remembered that his blue eyes had thick, dark lashes, like a girl's. He and Kegs held his arms while Trent started emptying stuff out of his backpack. When he saw the stun gun, the pickpocket's eyes bulged out of his head, and he wriggled when Trent wrapped duct tape around his mouth.

Jim had to admit he and Kegs were curious about the stun gun. They'd only seen them in video games, which was hardly real. Trent told us this SABRE model was the most powerful one on the market. The kid was bucking like a mule at this point. They held him down on the floor while Trent gave him the first jolt to the neck. He collapsed and a wet patch formed at his crotch.

"Eew, he pissed his pants," he'd said.

Kegs smacked the kid's head.

Trent gave the kid another jolt, this time in the groin. He let it go on for a long time, then said, "Have you learned your lesson yet?" Trent handed the hammer to Kegs. "Smash his goddamn hand."

"What? I'm not doing that, man."

"You suddenly scared? This little twerp is a damn thief. In Arab countries, they'd cut his hand off. Now, smash it hard, you wuss."

The kid was lying on the floor, nothing moving now except his frantic eyes. Trent held his arm out and unfurled his fingers. The kid looked directly at Kegs, as good old Kegs, his closest friend, raised the hammer and walloped it down into the middle of the kid's palm.

They heard a sickening crunch of bones. Tears sprang from the paralyzed young man's eyes.

Trent looked calmly at the scene and passed the hammer to him. "Your turn. Pickypocket's got two hands. What if he's a lefty? We don't want him stealing again, do we?"

"I'm not doing it," He'd said, looking over at Kegs, who wouldn't meet Jim's eyes.

"Kegs did his part. So did I. Are you going to be in this little fight club with us, or are you too good for that?" Trent gave the kid another long electric jolt in the arm and his head rolled to one side.

Jim didn't know exactly why he gave in, but it was for Kegs, not Trent. He didn't want to lose Kegs' friendship. Jim was angry, but he did it. He raised the hammer and smashed the poor kid's other hand.

He guessed it was too much for the scrawny body to take. The kid never came out of the paralysis. Maybe it was Jim's final blow. He'd never know, but the kid stopped breathing and went deathly still.

After the shock of realizing that they'd killed someone, Trent went into overdrive figuring out how to hide the body. He found a large plastic bag in a janitor's closet, enveloped the body, and wrapped tape around it to make it airtight. Then he looked around for someplace out of sight to stash the bundle. Trent made Jim, the strongest of the three, pry up the boards under the staircase. He was sweating from exertion and fear of discovery by the time the niche was opened up. Trent watched while Kegs mashed the parcel between the floor joists and nailed the boards and tile back on top.

Now, with Kegs dead, Jim was the only surviving witness who could describe Trent's role in that heartless murder. But just how valuable was his information? A Congressman running for U.S. Senate on a platform of helping the homeless had actually *killed* a homeless boy when he was a teenager? He had hidden the evidence, ordered Jim to dig it up years later, killed one of his accomplices, kidnapped the child of the other accomplice, and might just get caught red-handed trying to kill Jim himself.

Jim ran his fingers through his hair. How could he possibly pull this off? He never kidded himself about his own smarts. This operation would need a mission leader to organize it. Who could he get to help? Who could he trust who'd be willing to get involved? Especially after they heard about his role in the death of the homeless kid and the lumberjack.

Jim went through the contact list on his phone. He'd given golf lessons to a lot of high-powered people at the Country Club and had their cell phone numbers. Maybe one of them could help. Jim was all the way to the "S"s when he stopped at a name: Andy Shaw. The guy was a lousy golfer but, from gossip at the club, a shark of a criminal attorney. If Andy was willing to help, he'd surely be able to work out the logistics of how to rescue Jimmy while not getting father or son killed. And he could negotiate with the FBI for Jim to give evidence against Trent in order to reduce his time in prison.

Jim made the call and luckily, Andy Shaw, Esquire, answered it despite a lack of identification on caller ID. Criminal lawyers were probably used to clients calling them on burner phones. Jim filled him in on the basic story. Andy's gratitude for Jim's help in dramatically lowering his golf handicap may have factored into his agreement to take the case. They discussed the specifics of everything that had happened. At first, Andy was incredulous that Trent Westbrook's skeletons in the closet were literal ones, but Andy quickly switched into strategizing mode. After they went over every detail, Andy put together a plan.

Jim's new attorney called the head of the Nashville FBI Office to open negotiations on Jim's behalf. After a lot of back-and-forth, and discussion with the Massachusetts District Attorney's office, a deal was reached. Since Jimmy Jr.'s immediate safety was everyone's highest priority, it was decided that Jim would call Trent that night to offer himself up in an exchange.

The Nashville FBI chief sent over a pair of field agents to set up an untraceable phone tap for Jim's call. By ten p.m., flanked by two agents wearing headphones, Jim sat at his cramped kitchen table, fingers ready to punch in the number of Trent's secret burner phone.

59

Iris called Milo and Alise from Luc's car as he drove her home from the hospital. They were both relieved that Iris was safe and relatively sound. Milo assured her he'd welcome taking on anyone trying to mess with him now. Alise had the opposite reaction to Iris's warning. She decided to head up to a friend's cottage in New Hampshire for the week.

Sheba met her mistress in the entryway, wriggling with relief, aware that some unknown drama had taken place without her. They climbed upstairs to the loft and Luc headed to the kitchen to pour them each large glasses of buttery Montrachet. Iris chose one of her mellow playlists from her phone's Spotify app. It was Monday night. The restaurant was closed, and they were free to relax. Iris and Luc brought their wine into the living room and sprawled onto the sofa.

Iris paused for a moment, looking at her glass. "Am I allowed to drink yet? Have the drugs completely left my system?"

Luc asked, "How do you feel?"

"Still a little woozy."

"Better not take a chance." Luc took both of their glasses back to the kitchen and returned to the sofa with goblets of water. Just as Iris settled her head on his chest, the doorbell rang.

Reluctantly, they rose to check the video screen in the hall. Iris groaned when she saw it was Budge. She pressed the audio button. "Now is not a good time, Budge."

"Hear me out, Reid. Let me in for five minutes, and if you aren't interested in what I have to say, I'll leave. Promise." He flashed her a three-fingered Boy Scout salute.

Luc whispered in her ear. "Want me to get rid of him?"

She shrugged. "He did tell the cops I'd been kidnapped. I owe him. Better stay within earshot in case I decide to strangle him." She buzzed the reporter in.

"I'll be in the kitchen getting a start on dinner," Luc said. "Call if you need me."

When Budge arrived on the second floor, Iris asked, "How did you just happen to be in my neighborhood when I was kidnapped?"

He gave her a wide-eyed innocent look, a difficult trick to pull off if you looked uncannily like a toad. "Pretty lucky, right? Since you were ignoring my calls, I was trying to find you. After your podcast bombshell, I figured you'd want to expand on those remarks for the *Globe's* readers."

"Did you notice anything about the kidnappers or their car?"

"I was on the far side when their back door opened. Someone grabbed you and the car sped away. I did get the license plate but—"

"I heard. Stolen. Anyway, you said you had something interesting to say."

"Ever heard of Trent Westbrook?"

Iris kept her face blank. "The politician running for Senate? What about him?"

"Everyone thinks he's a great guy, championing the homeless and all. But I got a tip from a landlord in Somerville that Westbrook is behind a few real estate deals using a shell corporation to hide his ownership. He's been making under-the-counter donations to City

Councilors there, quietly getting the zoning laws changed to allow taller buildings and more lucrative projects."

"What a surprise—a sleazy politician. And this has what to do with me and what happened today?"

Budge's shrill voice continued, making Iris's head ache. "I started researching the guy and came across the fact that he'd gone to G&B for high school, right here in Cambridge. Since I happen to be the lead reporter on the paper's Little Jimmy Dugan story, I did some recon on Big Jim Dugan, the guy people say took the boy. Lo-and-behold, Jim Senior and sleazy Trent Westbrook were pals back at G&B."

Iris made a spinning get-on-with-it motion with her forefinger.

"I'm trying to put together a solid exposé on Westbrook with as much dirty laundry as I can find, ideally before his Senate election in two weeks. The paper's nervous about taking him on unless my story is airtight. So, if you've got something on Dugan, I would really like to know if it implicates Westbrook as well."

Iris considered. She'd told the FBI and Lieutenant Garcia about her suspicions. But who knew if either took them seriously enough to follow up. Budge had far more resources than she did to move her bits of information into meaningful action. She'd already been in real danger for letting some things slip out. Maybe she should let him run with the ball. She had to stop thinking of Budge as the annoying pest that he was in college, even though he was every bit as irritating now. He was a lead *Boston Globe* reporter, for God's sake. He could make people pay attention to the unsolved murders in *her* museum.

"Okay. I'll tell you what I have so far."

60

At ten p.m., Trent was smoking a fat Montecristo in his home office, his feet up on the desk when his cell phone rang. He reached for it, expecting an update from Edward, when he realized it was his other phone ringing. The secret burner. Finally, Jim had taken the bait.

Edward had gotten him a fancy untraceable phone with call recording, so Trent switched on the feature before punching "accept."

"Jimbo. Long time, no see. How are you doing?"

"You bastard. If you've touched a hair on Jimmy's head, I'll kill you!"

"Hey, hey. That's no way to talk to me." Trent kept his tone light. "We have some mutual business we need to discuss. Let's set up a time to meet."

"I want to talk to him."

"I can have someone text you a current photo. Everything's fine."

"You release him, then we meet."

"Jim, I'm sorry, but that's not how it works."

"What exactly is your proposal?"

"You in the area now?"

"Maybe."

"Be in Boston by tomorrow morning. At nine, I'll give you a call about where to meet and how it's going to work. Obviously, if any law enforcement is involved, Little Jimmy won't be coming home. That sound good?"

"No. Here's *my* condition. You drop Jimmy off at a fire station. I don't care where. Give him a phone so he can call my burner when he's safe. Once I hear from him, I'll turn myself over to you. And don't you hurt him, Trent, or I swear, you're dead!"

"Fine. I'll talk to you at nine." The call ended.

Trent speed-dialed Edward. "Dugan just called. He must be fairly close because he agreed to meet me tomorrow morning. So, he's not on a sailboat in Bimini."

"I always said he was still in the country, sir."

"Any sign of the boy?"

"They're still searching for him. Did Mr. Dugan ask for proof of life?"

"Yeah. I told him my associate would text him a photo. Did you get today's newspaper photo-shopped in?"

"It's all ready. I'll text it to his phone."

"He wants us to drop the kid off with a phone at a fire station. Any fire station. Jimmy calls his father's burner to say he's safe, then Dugan will turn himself over to us. Is that going to work with your plan? What if he's told the cops or the Feds?"

"Hmm. I think I can make that fit. We'll move Mr. Dugan from spot-to-spot tomorrow so no one can set up a trap in advance, and we can check out if anyone is following him. We'll tell him Jimmy will call him at the third location. When we're sure Mr. Dugan is alone, we'll eliminate him."

"You know this needs to be foolproof. It can't lead back to me."

"Understood, sir. Play back the conversation for me so I can see how you left it with him. I'll need to figure out the logistics and put together the team I want to use."

Trent replayed the call for Edward. Listening to it again, he congratulated himself in advance for getting this last loose end tied up.

61

Jimmy swept more leaves over his chest. He hoped the mud he'd smeared on his face would make him invisible in case the men looking for him swept their flashlights in his direction. He'd been cold when he first climbed out the window and started running through the woods, but he'd soon warmed up. After making his way through the dense forest for a while, he'd gotten a stitch in his side and stopped to hide. He wished he could have built a lean-to from branches like Bear Grylls on his favorite TV show would have done, but Jimmy could hear the men shouting in the distance, so he needed to try to blend in with the forest floor. The mud and leaves kept him warm enough.

It had been mid-afternoon on Sunday when the kidnappers had stopped their car near his driveway and asked him for directions to Cabot Park. Jimmy, brought up to be polite, had approached the car, which was so stupid because he *knew* not to talk to strangers. Mom would so mad.

The two kidnappers had removed Jimmy's mask when the car finally stopped. They were in a clearing in the middle of the woods, and it was very dark. The men had steered him into a cabin. He was really hungry, so they must have driven for many hours. It felt like midnight. One of the men, Jerry he thought his name was, heated up hot dogs for dinner. They had been nice enough to him. They all slept in the same little room on cots like at camp. The next day Jerry gave him a Game Boy to play with. It was some old-fashioned video game. After a few hours of trying to reach the top level, then reaching it, he had gotten bored. But there was nothing else to do, so he pretended to keep playing while he thought up an escape plan.

Lying on his back now, he looked up at the sky. The moon was a sliver and the stars seemed to pop. This was called a "dark sky", so Jimmy knew he was far from the lights of towns or cities. But that didn't mean there weren't farmhouses or roads with drivers who might stop for him.

The freckles of the Milky Way sprayed across the darkness. As Bear had instructed, Jimmy pictured the sky like a big clock, the type on his classroom wall at school. He searched for the Big Dipper and found it in the twelve o'clock position. The two stars on the end of the Dipper's cup led him to the North Star. There it was—just below the twelve o'clock position. Now he knew which way was north! From that discovery, it was easy to see that east was at three o'clock, south at six o'clock and west at nine o'clock.

Jimmy had been on enough family trips to know that travelling many hours south from Newton brought you to crowded places like New York City, not to deserted forests. Driving east took you into the ocean. So that meant that he was now either west or north of his home.

Jimmy would wait until the sounds of the searchers died down, then hike in a southeast direction. He had enough moonlight to avoid running into trees and would use the stars to point him toward safety.

Bear would be so proud of him.

62

Iris told Budge about the blue scrap of cloth snagged on the floor framing near Sam Parker's remains. She explained how this led her to conclude that his assailants had been students at G&B. Budge gave her a disbelieving look. When she told him how she'd identified the trio from the yearbook as Dugan, Westbrook, and a third boy, he snorted loudly.

"Remind me not to use you as a background researcher, Reid. That story is completely circumstantial. No hard connections."

Iris sat up in her chair, ready to argue, when he added, "However..."

She tried to restrain her annoyance.

"However, the fact that you were kidnapped, which I saw with my own eyes..." Budge tilted his head. "Unless you staged it?"

Her jaw set. "Why on earth would I do that? And the hospital verified I'd been drugged."

"Okay. Let's assume you were actually kidnapped. That, my friend, is the most convincing part of your argument. You'd just accused Dugan of being a person of interest in the museum murders. You claimed this on a podcast with five thousand listeners and who knows how much of a secondary audience." Budge cast his eyes up to the loft's ceiling. "Mighty fast reaction time on Dugan or Westbrook's part to arrange a kidnapping in an hour."

"I didn't say Dugan's name...exactly."

"Anyway, if either of those two were involved in the kidnapping, then that would for sure suggest a link to the murders. It's always the cover-up that gets the bad guys caught."

"How are we supposed to figure out who kidnapped me? You said you saw nothing useful."

"And you said you don't remember anything."

"They drugged me, okay?"

"What about before they drugged you?"

She must have struggled, Iris thought. She would have tried to use her karate skills. But it was the fingers on her right hand that suddenly pulsed. A memory came back to her in a flash. He was choking her. She couldn't breathe. She reached up her hands and scratched him on the face. A wave of panic washed over her, and she looked down at her nails.

Budge watched her. "What is it, Reid? Are you remembering something?"

"He was choking me. I scratched him on the face! Near his eyes, I think. Ugh, I may have his skin under my nails!"

Budge's eyes lit up. "You did? That's great! We need to get that analyzed for DNA. Unless the hospital already did that. We need to find out."

Iris stared at her hand. "I want to scrub my nails."

"No!" Budge screamed. "We need to get a forensics guy here to collect any evidence that's left."

Iris suppressed the urge to retch.

At that point, Luc came into the living room. "Everything all right in here?"

She looked over at him. "I need to call that FBI guy. Do you know where I left his card?"

Agent Kramer had been noncommittal on the phone when she'd told him about how she had scratched the kidnapper's face before he'd drugged her. "I'll check with the hospital to see if they thought to take nail scrapings. Even if we can get DNA from under your fingernails now, this guy may not be in our system. But if we catch someone, we can always check for scratches on his face. That may be evidence we can use."

Iris had tried to get Budge to leave in the interim, but he wanted to see if the forensics yielded anything useful. It hadn't helped that Luc offered him dinner, since Budge was a legendary mooch.

Agent Kramer reported that the hospital had neglected to scrape her nails for evidence, so he would bring over a technician to do it. Before the FBI agents arrived, Budge announced that he'd better wait in another room. "After I reported your abduction to the cops, Agent Kramer questioned me and clarified that I needed to keep a lid on any developments in the Little Jimmy case until they'd apprehended Dugan Senior. So, he won't want to see me here." Budge looked around the loft. "Where should I go?"

Iris paused, assessing which room would be less of a target for Budge's instinctive snooping. "You can wait in my home office." Most of her work equipment had already been moved to the new office, and they hadn't gotten around to converting the space into a guest room. She led Budge there, reassuring herself that nothing would capture his attention unless he wanted to flip through out-of-date window or plumbing fixture catalogs. Budge made himself at home, sitting in her old desk chair, focused intently on his phone.

She was impatient by the time Agent Kramer finally arrived at nine with an earnest young forensics technician in tow. Iris hadn't dared to touch anything for fear of destroying possible evidence. She had even tied a baggie around her hand to keep from further contaminating any evidence.

Iris brought the two men into the kitchen, where the lights could be turned up high. Luc watched from the dining room table on the far side of the kitchen counter. Iris sat on a stool and tried to breathe normally while the forensic tech examined her nails. As the young man took out a sharp scraping tool from a large case, Agent Kramer's phone rang. He walked into the hall where Iris could hear him murmuring. The conversation became inaudible as the agent retreated further down the hall.

The technician meticulously collected all possible traces of the kidnapper's skin from under her nails. Once he was finally finished, Iris ran to the bathroom to scrub her hand vigorously under hot water until it was red, using a nail brush to make sure any remaining skin from the kidnapper was gone. She passed Agent Kramer who was standing in the hall talking on his cell phone, and heard him say, "Good, we'll meet him when he lands tomorrow morning and wire him up inside the airport." He gave her a furtive look, turned away, and lowered his voice.

Shortly afterward, the FBI agents left, and Budge emerged from his hiding place, grinning like a naughty child.

"What are you so pleased about?" Iris asked.

Budge gave her a quick wave. "Thanks for dinner. Gotta go. Let me know if they match up any interesting DNA."

Hands on hips, Iris stood between Budge and the staircase. "Did you just eavesdrop on Agent Kramer's phone call? You know something. Let's have it."

"It's not eavesdropping if he has a clearly audible conversation outside the room where I'm checking my email and the door happens to be open a crack."

"Uh, huh. And what did you happen to overhear?"

Budge wavered between wanting to guard his precious scoop and wanting to brag about it. After a moment, he said, "The FBI has Dugan Senior. Sounds like he's being flown back to Norwood Airport tomorrow morning from wherever he's been hiding. They're wiring him up for sound in anticipation of an exchange with Westbrook for

Jimmy. So, turns out Dugan and Westbrook are indeed connected. Your crazy theory might just be true."

"I knew it! Didn't I tell you those two were in league? Now, we're getting somewhere. What time does their plane land?"

"Why? This is an FBI kidnapping case. You can't get involved. A kid's life is at stake."

"But you plan on being there, don't you?"

"Because Little Jimmy is *my* story! I need to be there for the emotional reunion. And *I* know how to keep my head down and not screw up a federal operation."

Before she could protest that she'd never screw up an op either, the image of her former employee, Roger, swam into her mind and she kept that thought to herself. "Dugan may have killed *my* carpenter as well as a poor, homeless guy who he stashed in *my* museum years ago. Westbrook may be the brains behind it. And one of them may have kidnapped me today. So, I have a personal stake in this. I'll stay well out of the way. Now, what time are we meeting tomorrow and where?"

63

About an hour before, Jimmy had heard a helicopter chuff-chuffing overhead, sweeping the woods with a bright light. He fell to the ground and spread leaves over himself until the noise of its engine died away. The night was really cold and even with all the running, he was shivering in his thin T-shirt. Jimmy didn't dare build a fire using the stick-rubbing trick he'd seen Bear do, because the smoke could attract the bad guys. He hadn't heard their voices for a long time, so maybe they'd given up looking for him. Still, he couldn't take a chance. The blanket of leaves warmed him up a little bit. He should just rest here for a while.

Sometime later, he didn't know when, Jimmy awoke to the sound of a loud snuffling noise nearby. The boy squinted open his eyes and stifled a gasp. An enormous black bear was rooting around under a tree nearby. It was using its long, sharp claws to scoop up acorns and shove them into its tan snout. The bear was facing sideways and probably hadn't noticed Jimmy yet.

He tried to remember the lesson about bears. Which one could you escape from by climbing a tree? A Black or a Brown Bear, or maybe a Grizzly? Did it matter? How could he get up from his messy cover of leaves without attracting its attention? All bears were fast runners and could catch him. The sky had already lightened to the pale gray of early morning, so he'd definitely be visible. Plus, he smelled sweaty. Didn't bears have a good sense of smell? He tried to glance around without moving his head. He didn't notice any cubs nearby, so that was a good thing.

Now he remembered. You were supposed to raise your arms high and wide to appear larger and yell in order to scare the bear, but a lot of good that would do. Jimmy weighed 50 pounds. The bear must weigh ten times as much. No way was a kid as small as he was, waving his arms around and shouting, going to signal anything other than *breakfast's here*.

The bear slowly started to turn. Jimmy felt his heart racing, remembering just in time to look away from the bear's eyes to avoid the risk of confronting him. He could see in his peripheral vision the bear lumbering toward him, closing the distance between them. He was so terrified he could barely breathe. He tried not to flinch as the bear's immense face hung over his, tried not to imagine those sharp teeth biting off his nose. The smell of peanut butter wafted toward him. Peanut butter? He kept his eyes closed tight, clenched his fists, and prayed harder than he'd ever done before.

Jimmy waited for what seemed like forever. He felt nothing and heard nothing. He finally opened his eyes, and the bear was gone. Its big rump was disappearing back into the deep woods. He cautiously rose and shook off the colorful leaves sticking to his sweaty shirt. After checking to be sure the bear hadn't circled back, he relieved himself against a tree. Was it time to eat some tree bark or bugs? He decided he wasn't all that hungry yet. He was thirsty, though, and cold. He needed to find someone soon who could help him.

There were no stars anymore, but the sun was rising in the east, so he could orient himself from that. The bear had headed north, thank goodness. He resumed walking in a southeast direction. The temperature had gone from cold to less cold. Jimmy rubbed his bare arms to warm them up.

After making his way through dense, colorful trees for what seemed like hours, but was probably less, he saw a clearing ahead. He ran eagerly toward it, hoping to find a road. Instead, he found a dirt track with faint tire marks. It must lead somewhere, and walking would be easier on this smooth surface. Maybe a car would come along. He followed it.

An hour later, he thought he heard the noise of a motor. He stopped to listen. It was a mechanical growl, like a truck, and it was definitely getting louder. Should he hide in case it was the bad guys looking for him? But if he ran over to the trees, he'd be too far away from the road to catch up to the truck by the time he decided it was safe. He would have to take a chance.

So, he placed himself bravely in the middle of the road, waving his arms, as a huge truck carrying an enormous load of logs sped toward him.

64

Budge picked up Iris the next morning at 7:30 a.m. in his tiny Fiat 500 with the Dartmouth sticker plastered across the back windshield. He was a fervent supporter of the college they had both attended. The sun was just rising. Halloween was two days away and by the time they'd left Cambridge, they'd passed countless intricately carved pumpkins and spider web covered porches in the morning haze.

"Are you taking Route 2 or the Pike?" Iris asked from the cramped passenger seat. Budge gave her a withering look, and she decided to leave the driving to him.

Five minutes later, he asked, "Did you bring coffee, Reid? Or muffins in your bag? You need to justify me letting you tag along."

"You wouldn't have even known about this development if you hadn't been at my house snooping."

Budge tipped his head in acknowledgement, and they sat in strained silence for the next half hour while Budge played road jockey with the other early-morning commuters on the Massachusetts Turnpike. Obedient to his Waze app, he turned south onto Route 128 and when he finally steered the Fiat off the exit toward Norwood, Iris asked, "What's the plan? How do we stay out of sight?"

"We follow the followers."

"Details?"

"I heard Agent Kramer said he would meet the FBI plane at the Norwood Airport at 8:25. This won't be where Westbrook's supposed exchange takes place. He probably told Dugan to get his ass to this area, then to expect a phone call at a specific time, to tell him where to meet and to arrive alone. Kramer will be listening in and will race to set up his people at the meeting site beforehand to blend into the background."

"Right. Like they do on TV."

Budge's eyebrows shot together. "You know, this story may not have a happy ending. This is clearly a trap. Westbrook won't want Dugan or Little Jimmy to survive, if the kid is even still alive. It will be up to Kramer to protect them. There'll probably be gunfire. So, we'll watch from a distance and keep our heads down. Understood?"

"I'm not naïve, Budge. I know this is a trap." Her cool tone belied the electric instincts setting all her nerves on edge. "I'm just hoping Agent Kramer can save the boy. I'd like to see both Dugan and Westbrook hauled off in handcuffs to answer for their crimes."

Budge pulled into the employee parking lot for the small airport next to a dinged Honda.

"I need to find a ladies room," Iris said.

"Wait. Kramer shouldn't see you. He can't know we're here."

She pulled out of her purse a baseball cap with a fall of blond hair attached. After fitting it on her head and donning sunglasses, she hopped out of the car and headed for the terminal.

65

Did the truck driver even see me? Jimmy wondered, as he scurried to the side of the road, still waving his arms. At least the old guy sitting high up in the driver's seat was not one of the kidnappers from the cabin.

The truck operator finally seemed to register that he had just seen a small boy and slammed on his brakes. The truck let out a loud hissing noise, shuddered, and came haltingly to a stop. Jimmy glanced at his mud-and-leaf-covered body and realized he must look a little scary.

The driver jumped down from the cab of the truck and strode around to stare at him. He was almost twice as tall as the boy and many times his weight. The giant shook his head and let out a long, piercing whistle. "Well, I'll be damned. What's a kid like you doing in the middle of Baxter State Park, all by yourself?"

Jimmy sized up the guy. He had a full white beard like Santa Claus, and his bulk reminded the boy of his father, so Jimmy decided to trust him. "I was kidnapped! Can you take me to the police, please? I want to go home."

The old guy removed his trucker hat and scratched his head of stringy white hair. His eyes grew wide. "Wait a minute. Ain't you that Little Jimmy kid who's been all over the news?"

Jimmy raised himself to his full three feet eight inches. "I'm *not* little!"

The rest happened in a blur. Gus, the truck driver, wrapped him in his cocoon-like parka and lifted him up into the truck. He handed Jimmy a bottle of water and a Snickers bar while he made some calls on his cell phone. Jimmy must have fallen asleep because the next thing he knew, he was lying on a cot in a police station. Gus and the truck were nowhere to be seen. The officers let him take a shower in their barracks and someone found him some clean sweatpants and a shirt that weren't too gigantic. Then they asked him the same questions again and again about the kidnappers and the cabin.

Jimmy didn't remember how long it was before his mother arrived. He learned he was in a town called Bangor in Maine, and that his mother was flying up in a special plane. When he saw her rushing down the hall toward him, he ran into her arms.

"Sorry, Mom. I know I shouldn't have gone up to that car. I forgot."

His mother was sobbing and running her hands over him, his face and chest, alternating with hugs, as if she couldn't believe he was real. Jimmy was embarrassed to find that he was crying too. He finally pulled away to seem less of a baby, but when he looked at the police people circled around them, he saw tears in their eyes too.

The yelling and commotion outside the station got louder. He could hear people calling, "Talk to us, Jimmy. Tell us your story."

He looked up worriedly at the police officer who seemed to be in charge.

"It's okay. It's just reporters. We're going to have a press conference as soon as the mayor gets here, and we'll answer their questions. Then you can go home with your mom."

66

As Iris approached the two-story terminal building, the side door of a white panel van slammed open. Two men in Kevlar vests with assault rifles hopped out and jogged through the glass doors. *Oh, they'll blend into the background big time.* She entered the terminal behind them. The men headed toward a stairwell, but an official-looking guy with an earpiece planted himself in front of the door, blocking Iris from following. It was just as well. She really did have to go to the ladies room.

Inside the stall, after Iris finished taking care of her immediate concerns, she thought she could hear muffled voices. There was a vent high up on the wall behind her. She stood on the toilet seat cover and put her ear close to it. She could clearly make out voices, probably from the room above her.

"Dugan's scheduled to land at 8:25. We'll bring him here, wire him up, and stake out his burner phone. Westbrook's supposed to call Dugan at 9:00 to tell him where to meet. Westbrook will be suspicious of outside interference, so he'll probably drag Dugan from place to place until he's certain that any tails have been shaken off.

This will make it hard for us to get you snipers into position ahead of time, so we're going to have to improvise."

The voice sounded like Special Agent Kramer. Iris heard murmurs of acknowledgement from the others.

"When do I get out of the back seat?" said a woman's voice.

"We'll be feeding intel to your earpiece, Monroe. Wait until I give you the word. Jenks, Coe and I will be in the van with the techs trying to follow."

Iris heard a cell phone chime. After a moment, she heard Agent Kramer say, "Oh, that's good news. And he's okay? They didn't harm him?"

Iris's mind raced. Did someone find Little Jimmy? Did this mean Dugan wouldn't go through with meeting Westbrook after all?

The agents voiced the same questions.

There was a minute of silence before Kramer went on. "Jimmy's been found safe. He escaped from a cabin in Maine and a logger found him. He doesn't know anything that would tie his kidnappers to Westbrook, but Dugan's conversation last night has Westbrook offering the kid in an exchange. Still, we're going to go through with this op using Dugan as bait. We need to catch Westbrook red-handed."

"Sir, are we going to tell Dugan that Jimmy's safe?" This was the woman's voice.

"I think not. I'm assuming that Westbrook won't tell him, and Dugan's not going to risk his neck unless it's to get his kid to safety."

"What happens if Dugan gets killed?"

"To our case?" Kramer said. "Dugan's filled out a sworn affidavit detailing everything that he and Westbrook have been involved in. His lawyer is holding it for the time being. Dugan is trading his testimony for a reduced sentence. But it's still better if we catch Westbrook in the act of attempted murder, so some slick lawyer can't claim Dugan is lying."

No one mentioned that catching Westbrook in the act of

attempted murder might not be as big a priority to Dugan as staying alive. He didn't get a vote.

Iris climbed down off the toilet and washed her hands while considering this new information. She was relieved that Jimmy was okay but felt bad for Dugan. He might not learn about his son's safety before getting taken out by Westbrook, or more likely, one of his henchmen. It seemed unethical.

She left the building and hurried over to the Fiat. Budge was in the middle of an animated phone conversation. She slipped back into the passenger seat.

He did a slow-motion double take before he recognized her in her wig, then ended the call.

"You'll never guess what's happened!" Iris said.

Budge slumped down in his seat. "Little Jimmy's been found and frickin' Marlene Grimes scooped me on the story."

67

Trent could not believe his bad luck. His men had not found the kid. Trent paced back and forth on the linoleum lobby floor of an empty brick building in Canton, thirty miles south of Boston. It was 8:30 a.m. and he was scheduled to call Jimbo at 9:00.

"If Jimmy gets rescued, can the damn kid tell them anything? I can't afford to have his disappearance traced back to me," he snapped at Edward, seated nearby sipping tea from a thermos.

"I doubt he's still alive, but we've stopped the search, cleared out the cabin, and sent Jerry and Tom away to lie low. They never mentioned your name in front of Jimmy." Edward took another sip of tea. "The bigger threat is if Mr. Dugan has involved law enforcement and tipped them off that you were behind taking the kid."

Trent threw up his hands. "How could he prove that? And what ever happened to mutually assured destruction? Jimbo stands to lose at least as much as me if he brings in the cops. *He* killed the carpenter and was involved in the other thing."

"The scales may have tipped for him when you took his kid, sir. And we both know that your good reputation, before next week's election, is critical now. But I hope I'm wrong. Mr. Dugan may follow your instructions and show up alone. In which case, everything is simple. We eliminate him and nothing can be proved about your involvement in any of this. I'm just trying to cover all the bases."

Trent stared out the window and narrowed his eyes. A group of three scruffy skateboarders had cruised into view on the terrace outside. They circled around, picking up speed, hopping up and down on the stone handrail and performing crazy jumps on the stairs. "There are damn kids out there! You said this place was deserted."

Edward rose and strode to the door.

Trent watched his fixer go speak to the skateboarders. After a brief discussion, followed by the teenagers' terrified looks and panicked flight, Trent felt sure they wouldn't be coming back anytime soon.

Edward strolled back into the building and calmly sat back down.

"What did you say to them?"

"That radioactive waste had recently been found here, and that they should go home immediately and take scaldingly hot showers to decontaminate themselves."

Trent smirked, glancing around the lobby, empty now of all furniture except a card table and a few mismatched chairs. He lowered himself into one of them. "What was this building used for, anyway?"

"A nursing home. It closed last year, and now it's on the market. No showings today. I made sure of that."

"Maybe I should turn it into one of my homeless shelters. I'm going to make a killing on those. Or rather, my shell companies will."

"Better to leave this one alone, since it will be the place where Mr. Dugan meets his maker. We'll plant him out back, deep. We don't want any links to you."

Trent stroked his chin. "Okay, let's talk contingencies. What's the plan if Jimbo arrives with the feds or cops?"

"I'm running him through a sieve before he gets here. I have people set up at the various stops to pick off any followers." Edward took out a piece of paper from his jacket pocket and handed it to

Trent. "Each time Dugan phones in, you're going to send him to both of these locations where he'll wait for your next call before ending up here. Remind him that if we see any sign that he's not alone, he'll never see his son again. I'll be monitoring reports from my people along the route, and we'll make any necessary adjustments. As soon as Mr. Dugan gets out of his car, I'll do the final honors myself, but our two assets from the first stop will be here by then as backup. This property has total visual privacy, and no one will hear a gun with a silencer."

Edward's icy blue eyes looked past Trent into the middle distance. "You can leave before he gets here or stay for the finale. Your choice."

68

Iris slipped off her wig and checked her phone to see if any news about Little Jimmy's escape had hit the news outlets yet. She glanced over at Budge, still sulking in the cramped driver's seat of his car. "You took a gamble and lost," she said. "Shit happens. Focus on the Dugan story and move on."

Budge gave her a death glare. "Unlikely to be a front-pager. I'm sure Big Jim doesn't have an angelic gap-toothed smile like his kid."

"Maybe you'll get lucky, and the FBI will blow something up. And weren't you pursuing dirt on Trent Westbrook? If the FBI manages to implicate him today, that should be a huge story."

"You don't understand journalism, Reid. A rescued gap-toothed kid trumps a run-of-the-mill dirty politician any day. The latter are a dime a dozen. People just yawn."

The hoarse whine of a distant engine interrupted their discussion. It gradually got louder.

Budge reached over Iris's knee toward the glove compartment. "Don't get excited, Reid. I'm not getting fresh." He took out a pair of binoculars and searched the skies. "Private plane coming in on our right," he announced.

Iris squinted and picked out the quickly growing speck. Her phone read 8:22. "Must be Dugan. There's not much air traffic at this hour."

They watched the aircraft make its approach and touch down expertly on the landing strip. It had no special FBI markings.

"Cessna Citation. The FBI likes to use them for surveillance," Budge announced.

"Surveillance in this country?"

"Oh, right. We don't do that here." Budge twisted around and grabbed an elaborate camera with a long lens from the back seat.

Iris held her phone in front of her with its camera app open and pinch-enlarged the picture to get a close-up of their quarry.

The door to the plane opened and a man in a dark suit and sunglasses climbed down the short set of steps and waited. Next, a man built like a linebacker emerged, ducking his head at the doorway. His face looked tan, and his strawberry blond hair looked longer than in his photos in the paper. But it was definitely James Dugan Senior who'd just exited the plane, followed by a second agent.

Budge, who had cheered up considerably, took a fast series of photographs of Dugan. "This op is now in play."

The three men headed for the terminal. Dugan looked sick with worry. Iris tried to send him a mental message that his son was okay.

69

Jimmy sat uncomfortably on a raised platform that had been set up outside the Bangor police headquarters, with his mother on one side and the nice head police guy, Lieutenant Brewster on the other. A crowd of reporters and TV cameras were lined up in front of them. He wished he wasn't wearing stupid borrowed clothes. Would the kids at school see him like this? His mom was holding his hand, but that was hidden behind a table, so he didn't let go.

A man in a suit, the mayor he guessed, praised the police for rescuing Jimmy in such difficult terrain and bringing the boy to safety. Lieutenant Brewster coughed and corrected the mayor. "Jimmy rescued himself by courageously escaping from his captors and hiding all night in the woods in sub-freezing temperature. In the morning, he walked eight miles before he found a logging trail. He attracted the attention of a truck driver who brought him the last stretch to a police station. I can't stress enough what a brave and resourceful boy Jimmy Dugan is."

A reporter shouted out, "Why was he kidnapped?"

The lieutenant answered, "We're working with the FBI to try to find that out. Jimmy's father is missing, and the cases may be related. That's all I can say right now."

What did that mean? His mom had said that his dad had to go away for a while. Were the bad guys after him, too? Was his dad safe? Jimmy anxiously chewed on his lower lip.

"Jimmy, how did you stay warm at night or know what direction to walk?" a lady with yellow hair and a microphone asked.

"I just remembered what Bear on TV told us to do."

"Bear? You mean a cartoon show, Smokey the Bear?"

"No-o-o! Bear Grylls! My favorite show. It's on the Disney channel. He tells you how to survive in the wilderness. Like to get under a blanket of leaves and mud to keep warm, and how to use the North Star to show you which way to walk home. I had to guess that I needed to walk southwest. Then, a real bear found me when I was sleeping, but I couldn't remember what to do."

At this, his mother gripped his arm, her face white. He turned to her. "But I didn't move. The bear came right up to me, but I didn't look him in the eye, and he left me alone."

A buzz rose from the reporters. Jimmy heard someone say, "The kid escaped from a bear? Is he putting us on? Is this a hoax?"

Lieutenant Brewster stepped back up to the microphone. "The Rangers in Baxter State Park reported that a large male black bear broke into a cabin last night and ransacked the pantry. He finished off several tins of tuna fish and some large tubs of peanut butter. So, Jimmy is a lucky boy as well as a smart one. It appears that this bear's stomach was good and full when he encountered a muddy boy hiding in the leaves. Now it's time to let Jimmy go home with his mom to get some well-deserved rest."

As Jimmy was ushered back inside the station, he asked his mom, "Do you think Dad will come back now if he sees me on TV?

70

Spending an hour cooped up in a tiny car with Budge Buchanan was Iris's idea of hell. She tried to get out to pace around the airport parking lot, but Budge grabbed her arm.

"We can't risk Kramer seeing you, even in a stupid wig. Surveillance 101: stay hidden inside the damn car. Why do you think we journalists keep pee jars with us? We're like cops." Budge turned to look in the back seat for one, but Iris put up a hand.

"Don't even think about using one of those while I'm trapped in here with you."

Budge shook his head in disgust. "What kind of Dartmouth grad are you? Didn't you go on Freshman Orientation week?"

"Where they teach you to pee in a bottle with other people nearby? A valuable life skill. How did I miss that?"

Budge turned his attention back to his phone. After a minute, he started muttering. "The kid just had a press conference. Turns out he knows wilderness tricks and survived a close encounter with a bear. Unbelievable! This should be *my* story!"

Iris ignored him. She had finished the Spelling Bee and Wordle on her phone and was scrolling through the rest of the NYTimes site for more puzzles when a call came in from Luc.

"So, how's the stakeout going? Did the guy show up?"

"Dugan got here and is inside the airport building." Iris checked the time on the upper corner of her phone. 8:50. "The kidnappers should be calling soon to tell him where they want to meet. We'll stay far away from danger."

"I'll hold you to that. You promised you'd stay in the car with Budge." Luc continued, "I don't know if I can go through another day like yesterday."

She felt warm inside. It felt good to have someone concerned about her. "Don't worry. I have no intention of taking any risks today."

After Iris ended her call, Budge glanced over. "This kid Jimmy is a celebrity. I wonder if Dugan could get me an exclusive interview with him if I manage to save his life today."

"You thinking of interfering in an FBI operation? What happened to Surveillance 101: stay hidden inside the damn car?"

"If an opportunity presents itself—"

Iris cut him off. "Look, they're coming out."

Agent Kramer led Dugan toward an old gray Kia. The two men spoke briefly while a short female agent climbed into the back seat, crouched down in the footwell, and pulled a dark blanket over her head. Dugan folded himself into the driver's seat and backed out the Kia. He headed for the exit while Kramer and the snipers boarded the van.

Budge waited several moments before he started the Fiat.

As the stream of cars maneuvered onto Rt. 128 South, the van's resemblance to a giant marshmallow made it easy to follow from eight vehicles behind. But the gray Kia was somewhere out of sight.

"You'd think the FBI would disguise their surveillance vehicles better," Iris said. "Where do you guess Westbrook is sending Dugan?"

"Most likely, to a secluded spot so he can see if anyone is following."

The van moved into the right-hand lane and its blinker suggested a turn at the next exit.

"Route 24? Dugan's going to Rhode Island?"

"Reid, you're really getting on my nerves. I don't need a soundtrack."

Iris tried to change the channel on her thoughts, but she kept imagining Dugan being led to the slaughter. How could the FBI protect him from a hidden sniper's bullet?

Minutes crawled by before she spoke again. "The van's getting off at the Stoughton exit. I wonder if Dugan's going to Ikea? They have a huge parking lot. The store doesn't open until 10:00, so there won't be many people around."

Budge made a noncommittal grunt.

"Unless they're going to the restaurant first to get some meatballs for breakfast. That section opens at 9:30." She couldn't stop babbling.

The van turned right onto Ikea Boulevard. Budge accelerated to make the light. The two cars in front of him peeled off into the Christmas Tree Store driveway and they found themselves exposed, directly behind the van.

Budge swore under his breath.

"The gray Kia's heading into the Ikea parking lot," Iris said smugly.

The van, using no blinkers, turned quickly into the Yankee Candle store parking lot. Budge continued straight ahead.

"We're getting too close to Dugan's car!"

"I've got no choice. I don't want the van to notice us."

71

There was no place for Budge to peel off, so they ended up following Dugan into the vast covered parking lot. In the far corner, away from the store's entrance, he pulled into a space near a black Honda Accord. Budge passed him and headed toward the small group of cars already clustered by the sliding glass doors. He positioned his Fiat to face the corner where Dugan was parked and grabbed his binoculars from their cockeyed perch in the cup holder.

"Are you sure Westbrook's men can't see us?" Iris asked.

"Look around. Is anyone watching us? Someone must be keeping an eye on Dugan."

Iris studied the side mirror, shifting it around to get different angles, and noticed a gap in the atrium curtains on the store's second floor. Surely there wouldn't be a sniper positioned in the Ikea kitchen cabinet department. But if that was one of Westbrook's henchmen, he had a clear view of Dugan's car. Their Fiat, parked directly below, shielded its inhabitants from view.

She used her phone's camera again to zoom in on Dugan and could see him talking on his phone. The large man emerged from his car and walked over to the Honda. He squatted down by its front tire and appeared to retrieve an object hidden in the wheel well. He opened the driver's door, lifted out a small backpack from the seat and set it down on the pavement. Then he started unbuttoning his shirt.

"What's he doing?" Iris asked.

Budge let out a low whistle. "Smooth move. Westbrook must be making him undress."

"In a parking lot?"

"Someone's obviously watching him, looking for a wire. And it doesn't look like he's got one under his shirt. But there could have been a device sewn into his clothes or in his shoes."

When Dugan had stripped down to his boxers, he held up his hands and rotated around a full 360 degrees, leaving the middle finger of his right hand upraised. He lowered his hands, turned away from the building and quickly switched his underwear with a pair from the bag.

Iris glanced in the side mirror again to check the store's second-floor window. She thought she saw a glint of light, hopefully binoculars, not the reflection from a gun. Since the windows were inoperable, the sniper would have to cut out a small circle of glass for the gun like Iris had seen done in movies. It would be especially humiliating to be shot wearing just your underwear.

Dugan lifted a sweatsuit out of the bag and pulled it on.

Didn't anyone else notice a man stripping down in the parking lot? Iris surveyed the employees hurrying into the store to clock in and the savvy consumers hoping to get a jump on their shopping by entering through the restaurant. None paid a bit of attention to the crazy guy, probably off his meds, a hundred yards away.

Dugan finally removed his shoes, left them on the pavement, and got into the Honda barefoot.

Budge shook his head and said, admiration in his voice, "Westbrook has thought of everything. Dugan may just be screwed."

Iris lowered her phone and glared at him.

In another few seconds Dugan backed the Honda out of its

parking space and navigated toward the exit, leaving the Kia and a pile of clothes behind. Iris took a photo of the new car's license plate as it passed.

"So much for the agent in the back seat," Budge said.

Instead of continuing on along the exit road, the black car took a sudden sharp right onto a tiny lane marked *emergency vehicles only.*

Iris searched for Agent Kramer's number in her contact list as Budge trailed the Honda at a discrete distance.

"Wait. Are you calling Kramer?" Budge asked. "We don't want him to know we followed Dugan. We could get in big trouble."

Iris hesitated. "But Dugan might not have any protection unless we tell the agents the new car's license plate. She pressed the speed dial and was sent straight to voicemail. "Damn! He may not pick up messages while he's on an active operation." She left him a message with the photo of the new car's plate.

"As a serious journalist, I could get in so much trouble for becoming part of the story." Budge sighed. "Do you see the van anywhere?"

Iris scanned the road behind them. "Nope. Does this mean we're Dugan's only cavalry?" She glanced at Budge's profile, all tense with beads of sweat forming on his forehead.

72

Trent sat in the former nursing home lobby watching his Chief of Security orchestrate this impressive operation. Edward sat at the card table across from Trent, eyes focused on multiple screens, communicating with his underlings through a Bluetooth headset. He was meticulously tracking Jimbo's progress into the center of the trap.

"There was an agent hidden in the car?" Edward said to one of his spies. "She grabbed the clothes and drove off before you got there? Doesn't matter. I assumed Dugan would pull something like this. Did you catch the trail car? A Fiat 500? Seriously? That doesn't sound like the feds. But Jorge can intercept it at the next stop." Edward got up to stretch his long legs. "You and Mike should head over here now to meet us at the Canton location and take up your stations. Good work, so far."

Trent tried to feel some sympathy for Jimbo, his old high school buddy, outsmarted once again. Jimbo, and Kegs before him, were born followers, useful until they weren't. He tried to remember the details from that night in Harvard Square, twenty years earlier. The whole thing had been a dumb-ass teenage prank. The pot dealer had stolen his wallet and Trent and his friends wanted to teach the punk a lesson. But it had gotten out of control. Kegs and Jimbo were the ones who had crushed the kid's hands. The pain was probably what killed him. Or the kid might have had a heart attack. No reason for Trent's involvement in a youthful mistake to derail what was now a promising career in politics. Look at Teddy Kennedy and Mary Jo Kopechne.

Twenty minutes ago, it had been a shock to learn that Jimbo's kid had been found. But after Edward's reassurance that Jimmy's kidnapping couldn't be traced back to Trent, he felt some relief that killing the boy hadn't been necessary. After all, he wasn't a monster. Kegs and Jimbo had been direct threats to his future, but Jimmy hadn't done anything to him. The unfortunate murders he'd been involved with were on the same moral level as killings in battle. The last eight days had done nothing to alter that conviction.

"Dugan's passing the Holy Ghost Fire Anointing Church now, Jorge," Edward said. "He should be pulling into the warehouse in ten minutes. Tell Smitty to look out for a green Fiat 500 or any other tails. Dugan needs to be completely clean by the time he's headed towards us. You got that?"

Edward ended the call and looked up at his boss. "So, you've decided to stay for the finale?"

73

Iris tried to keep Dugan's new black car in sight while Budge's Fiat crept along behind an enormous minivan with three kids in the back seat twisted around to make faces at Budge.

"It figures the bad guys would pick the most common car brand and color in Massachusetts for us to try to follow," he muttered.

"I'm in constant awe of your knowledge of useful facts. Hey look. That big, old brick building is called the Holy Ghost Fire Anointing Church. Great name."

"Eyes on the target, Reid! We're not here to sightsee."

"I'm watching. The Honda's four cars ahead." Iris spotted the sign for a Starbucks and thought wistfully of how good a tall latte would taste about now. The bulky minivan turned off at a dentist's office and Budge slowed to allow a station wagon to pull out of the next driveway to take its place in line.

Iris kept her eyes trained on Dugan's car as her mind wandered to thoughts about what type of person he might actually be. According to Judith, the night Sam disappeared, three young men dragged her homeless friend away. Chances were, Dugan was one of those three involved in Sam's murder. Recent evidence also pointed to Dugan being the one who killed Carl on Iris's museum construction site. She could still picture the procession of motorcycles wending its way behind a distraught Milo from Carl's funeral to the cemetary.

But Dugan was now offering himself up as a sacrifice so that his son might be freed. He must know that Trent Westbrook had no intention of letting him live. Maybe Dugan was drawn into one really bad deed when young, and then, years later, Trent blackmailed him into returning to the crime scene to remove the evidence, compounding his crimes. But how do you justify murder?

Luckily, it wasn't Iris's job to decide the nature and degree of Dugan's guilt. And if she and Budge couldn't somehow help keep Dugan alive, it would be a moot point.

"The Honda's turning right up at the McDonald's," Iris said.

"Got it. I think we're crossing into Canton now. Do you know this area?"

"Other than the turnoff to Ikea from the highway, not at all. It looks more industrial." The road was curvy, and the speed limit dropped to a crawling 20 mph. The station wagon in front of them turned off at a garden center, leaving a single car between the Fiat and the Honda.

"We look very exposed here. Is there anyway to fall back?" Iris said. "Wait, he's turning right into that driveway leading to a warehouse. Go past him."

Budge let out an irritated snort. "Planning to." He drove on. A sign appeared for the Canton Ice House and he pulled into a busy parking lot in front of an enormous skating rink enclosure. He wedged his tiny car between two hulking SUVs, facing the direction in which Dugan had headed. A row of bushes shielded all but the Fiat's front windshield and roof from view.

As Budge reached for his binoculars, Iris pointed. "Over there. The Honda's stopped in front of the warehouse."

The big, overhead garage door jerked slowly open, revealing an interior shrouded in shadow. Dugan's car crept ahead and was quickly swallowed up inside.

74

"Now that Dugan's out of sight," Iris said, "they might kill him! We have to do something."

A vein visibly throbbed on the side of Budge's forehead. "Call Kramer again."

Iris punched his contact button. She reached a recording again and left word about Dugan's present location inside a warehouse, adding that Agent Kramer needed this information without delay. Hopefully, an agent monitored his messages while he was busy on an operation. She didn't leave her name or Budge's, but the FBI could easily trace the call if they wanted to find them.

As much as Iris was tempted to leap out of the car and break into the warehouse, recklessness would not help Dugan and would probably get her killed. Why did she have this compulsion to try to save people? Dugan wasn't even an innocent guy. But the DA and the court system should mete out justice, not Trent Westbrook's thugs.

She gripped Budge's arm. "How soon will Kramer's agents get here? Do you think they'll use a helicopter?"

He lowered his binoculars and looked pointedly at her hand on his arm.

She let him go and cracked her window open. "Did you hear a gunshot?"

"They'd use a silencer."

As the minutes ticked by, the tension in the claustrophobic car became palpable. Suddenly, the garage door started to rise. Budge and Iris leaned forward in their seats, looking through binoculars and the zoom on Iris's phone, as a front bumper appeared. Iris jotted down this new car's license plate and sent it to Agent Kramer in a text.

A navy-blue Toyota hatchback pulled out into view. Budge was the first to recognize the driver. "It's Dugan. He's still alive."

Iris let out her breath, then looked at him. "I don't get it. Is Westbrook actually going to let Dugan live?"

Budge shook his head. "He's making sure to eliminate any tails. He keeps making Dugan change cars while his lookouts check for anyone following him."

"But that means...?"

"If they noticed us following the Kia and the Honda, they'll want to get rid of us," Budge's voice was shaky.

"We need to get out of here fast!"

When Budge tried to back up the car, a large SUV pulled up behind, blocking him in. A beefy-looking man, with one hand ominously shoved into his pocket, jumped out of the car and approached the passenger side of the Fiat. He opened the door before it occurred to Budge to lock it and squatted next to Iris. He pointed a very long gun at her head.

"Out, you two. Get in this car."

75

Trent was eager to get this unpleasant task finished up so he could go back to his office and freshen up before his afternoon visit to an assisted living facility in Medford. But judging from Edward's expression as he spoke to some unknown asset on his Bluetooth, something had gone wrong.

"Why didn't you take them back to the warehouse?" Edward asked. "You could have disposed of them there, out of sight."

They? FBI agents?

"Fine." Edward's mouth looked pinched. "Bring them here. I'll have dealt with Dugan by the time you arrive. And Jorge, you told him he'll get the phone call from his son as soon as he parks and enters the lobby, right? Okay." When Edward ended the conversation, his right hand was clenching and unclenching rhythmically.

"What happened?" Trent demanded.

Edward's features shifted back into a more composed look. "After they sent Dugan off in the third car, Jorge and Smitty intercepted the green Fiat near the warehouse. *The Globe* reporter who's been pestering you and that architect we picked up yesterday were inside. Jorge's bringing them here."

Trent tried to puzzle out this new information. "What are those two doing together? And how did they know about Dugan's arrival in the area? Are we sure the FBI lost his trail?"

Edward stood, held up a hand, and started to pace around the lobby. "I need to think."

He made several loops up and down the space before retaking the seat next to Trent. "This doesn't change the plan for disposing of Dugan." Edward consulted his watch. "I need to get into position now. We keep it simple with the other two. I'll pick them off when they get out of Jorge's car, same as with Dugan. We can bury all three together. They'll just disappear."

Wait a minute. Two extra casualties? "Isn't that body count going to raise suspicions? Someone's going to notice a missing reporter and architect."

"But if their bodies are never found, law enforcement can't make a case for murder. Maybe they were lovers who ran off or made a suicide pact."

Trent pursed his lips. "Good point. Proceed."

Edward lifted the AR-15 rifle out of its case, loaded a full clip of ammunition, and headed out to the woods next to the parking lot.

Thank God my fixer can think on his feet. But when did he stop calling me 'sir'?

76

Jim Dugan spotted the sign on his left for the Riverbend Country Club. He drove along the quiet road, passing a large golf course, and glanced over at it. Not many players on a Tuesday morning. He pulled into the club's main entrance and parked the Toyota in the member's parking lot. Jim rested his head on the steering wheel and took some deep breaths. Time to play his last card.

He punched in Trent's number and started to speak as soon as Trent picked up. "I forgot to mention that I detailed everything that happened to that homeless kid twenty years ago. Everything you did to him, stunning him to death. I left a sworn affidavit with my lawyer, who will take it to the FBI and the media if I don't make it home today, with my son. I also suggested that the police reopen the investigation into Keg's death, since he was the other witness to your crime. How do you think that news will go over with the voters?"

Trent's voice rose half an octave. "You've got it wrong, Jimbo. You and Kegs smashed the boy's hands. That's how he died. I was just a horrified witness. And you killed that carpenter. You'll go to jail. Jimmy won't have his father around to see him grow up. You've been on the run. Who are the cops going to believe?"

"Let's let a jury decide."

Then Jim let the silence sink in until Trent spoke again. "You don't need to threaten me. We made a deal and I'll stick to it. As soon as you get here, you can speak to Jimmy. He should be home by then. Just follow the directions I gave you. Where are you now?"

77

Iris and Budge exchanged fraught looks as they sat in the back seat of the SUV with Beefy, Iris squeezed in the middle. The driver was talking softly, inaudibly, into his Bluetooth microphone.

"Where are you taking us?" Iris said. "Our kids will get out of their skating lesson any minute. If we're not there, they'll raise an alarm. You need to take us back!"

Beefy looked at her evenly and said nothing. His gun sat on his lap, the silencer aimed in their general direction. His trigger finger was within a split-second reach.

Then she noticed the scratch marks across his left cheek and smiled ruefully. This was the man who'd grabbed her in front of the museum yesterday. She'd made those marks before he had chloroformed her. No way would she convince him he'd picked up the wrong anonymous bystanders.

Budge tried a different approach. "Look, you've taken our wallets and know I'm a reporter. I got a tip that Dugan was arriving back in town, and just want to interview him. My friend is along for the ride. You don't need to keep us. We don't know anything. Take us back to our car. No harm, no foul. The *Boston Globe* knows where we were. You guys don't want them doing a Spotlight feature on you, do you?"

This argument had as little effect on Beefy as hers had. They passed a sign announcing the Riverbend Country Club up ahead. The driver veered off onto a dirt road which skirted the back of the property. There, the golf course met a wooded area. An even-narrower access road branched off into the woods, and the driver slowed down to maneuver the large SUV onto it.

This was ominous. Once kidnappers had you in their car, the odds for survival were dismally low. And when they drove you to a secluded part of the woods, you'd reached the fight-or-be-killed-stage.

But those odds didn't take into account Iris's brown belt in karate. Uechiryi, her style of martial art, encouraged close-in fighting. Still, having Beefy sitting thigh-to-thigh with her presented some maneuvering challenges. And she'd need to keep Budge out of her way.

Should she wait until they were out of the car? Better disarm Beefy while the driver was still paying attention to the road. Too bad she couldn't count on Budge to wrap the driver in a headlock. She'd have to make sure both of them stayed out of her way.

Iris caught Budge's eye. She tipped her head toward Beefy and pointed her thumb subtly at her own chest. She mouthed "fight." His eyes widened.

She started taking sharp, noisy intakes of breath, known as Sanchin breathing in Uechiryi. This was as much to attract Beefy's attention and get him to lift the gun a few inches, as it was to fill her lungs. Her pulse started to hammer. Beefy, curious as expected, twisted to see what she was doing. Off-balance, his weight was shifted awkwardly to the side and his gun hand rose. Lightning fast, Iris drove her right elbow, supported by her left fist directly down into his groin. *Not original, but all she could manage in the confined space.*

He let out a sharp canine howl. Both of Beefy's hands grabbed the injured area as he doubled over in agony. The gun slipped to the floor. Iris grabbed it and handed it over to Budge who held it awkwardly. The driver slammed on his brakes and glared at her in the rearview mirror. But before he could move, Iris clapped her hands hard over both of his ears from behind, almost hearing the explosion that must have caused inside his head. He collapsed, clutched his ears and moaned.

She shoved Budge's shoulder. "Run!"

"Doors are locked," he protested.

Iris pointed at the driver's door. "Press the button. The childproof lock."

The driver was still leaning over. Budge reached behind him and released the locks. Budge stowed the gun in the back waistband of his pants as he jumped out of the car. Iris slid out after him and ran around the SUV to the front passenger door. She scooped up their wallets and phones from the front seat and shoved them into her purse. Iris slung it over a shoulder and ran after Budge into the woods.

She could hear his heavy breathing in front of her. After a few minutes, he was wheezing. Iris tapped his shoulder. "Stop for a second. They should be out of commission for a while." She grabbed her phone from her purse and left another message for Agent Kramer, describing Dugan's new navy Toyota hatchback. She also told him where, if they acted quickly, they'd find the two men who'd just tried to kidnap them in the woods behind the Riverbend Country Club.

Budge was leaning against a tree, taking deep breaths.

"You okay? We should probably get going again."

He nodded, and they jogged on until they reached the edge of the golf course. There were no golfers in sight, so they committed heresy by walking on the greens in their civilian shoes. *Hell, this is a life and death situation.*

Soon, a large Shingle-style building rose before them like a mirage.

"I don't know about you, but I'm heading to that clubhouse to call an Uber to take me home," Iris said. "Dugan's on his own. Good luck with your story."

"I'm with you. No article is worth getting killed for. We're probably in deep shit with Agent Kramer over our involvement so far. We don't need to get in any more trouble."

They trudged across a vast parking lot toward the building. Iris checked behind her to see if Beefy and the driver were pursuing them. In her peripheral vision, she caught sight of a navy Toyota hatchback in the middle of a row of cars. She glanced at the side window as they got closer and recognized a familiar profile. "Oh, my God. It's Dugan."

78

Iris approached Dugan's car. She could feel Budge's hand on her shoulder.

"Uh, what did we just agree on, Iris?"

Ignoring Budge, she waved at Dugan and mimed rolling down his window.

Jim Dugan looked at her, alarmed. He flapped a hand in a go-away motion.

"I just want to talk," she said loudly enough to be heard through the closed window.

He shook his head emphatically and turned on his engine.

Iris ran around and stood behind his car so he couldn't get out of his parking space without doing an eighteen-point turn. Or running her over.

Budge tried to pull her away. "Are you nuts?"

"*He's* not the one who's been trying to kill us," Iris hissed, forgetting for the moment about the fugitive's alleged crimes.

Dugan opened his door, got out of the car, and stood up straight. He was a giant! He certainly looked menacing as he took several steps toward her. "I don't know who you are, but you're endangering my son. Get out of the way or I'll run you over."

So much for him not trying to kill me.

"Your son is safe. He escaped from Trent Westbrook this morning," Iris said.

Dugan's mouth hung open. "Wait. Are you FBI?"

"No. It's a long story how we're involved, but your son's escape has been on all the media channels. I can show you on my phone."

Dugan approached her cautiously. "This better not be a trick."

Iris scrolled to the *bostonglobe.com* and turned her phone so he could see the screen. The lead story was **Little Jimmy Rescues Self from Freezing Temperatures and Bear in Maine Wilderness.** A photo showed the grinning boy being embraced by his mother. Dugan read the entire article, swearing quietly under his breath. Iris noticed Budge surreptitiously taking a photo with his own phone of the preoccupied man.

Dugan's lips pressed together tightly when he handed the phone back to Iris. "This says Jimmy was at a police station in Maine early this morning. The FBI would have known that."

Iris averted her gaze. "We know nothing about the FBI's decisions."

Budge now stepped forward with a hand extended. "Hi, Jim. I'm Robert Buchanan from the *Boston Globe*."

Dugan stepped back, and Budge dropped his hand. "I've been writing about your son's kidnapping and have been hoping for a happy ending like this."

Dugan gave him a skeptical look. "Yeah, I've seen what you reporters have said about me." He turned to Iris. "And I recognize you now. You're that architect who told everyone that I killed both guys who were found in your museum."

Budge ventured that favorite line of reporters: "Why don't you tell us your side of the story? Tell us what really happened, and we can correct the record."

The squeal of tires on asphalt distracted Iris. She saw a large, white van racing into the parking lot, followed by a gray Kia. "We've got company."

They froze in place as they registered the dramatic arrival of the FBI van.

Did my helpful messages to Kramer outweigh my interference in an FBI operation?

Before the van even skidded to a full stop, the side door slid open. Agent Kramer stepped out and glared at them, gray eyes sharp, mouth a tight line. The pair of snipers in Kevlar vests flanked him, their assault rifles aimed at Budge.

Iris felt the color drain from her cheeks. "Did you pick up the two men in the woods?" Iris asked timidly.

Kramer ignored her question. "Ms. Reid and Mr. Buchanan, turn around and put your hands on the car."

They followed directions. Dugan moved away from them out of the line of fire.

"Mr. Buchanan, carefully remove the gun from your waistband with two fingers and place it on the ground."

"Sorry, I forgot I had that." Budge called over his shoulder. "It belongs to one of those two men in the woods. The big guy."

Kramer continued, "Slowly kick the gun toward me. That's right. Do you have any more weapons on you?"

Budge shook his head.

"Now, Ms. Reid, do *you* have any weapons?"

Iris shook her head. "Can we put our hands down now?"

Kramer picked up the gun from the asphalt and stuck it in his own waistband. Then he turned to Iris and Budge. "What part of 'do not interfere with an FBI investigation' did you two not understand?"

Budge's attention seemed to be fixed on the ground. "I'm sorry. We meant to stay out of the way."

Iris added, "We were just trying to help you catch the guys who kidnapped me yesterday. Maybe you noticed the scratches on the big guy's cheek? I made those." She held up her scraggly fingernails. "We figured Budge's little car wouldn't look like law enforcement following Mr. Dugan. And when we noticed him switching vehicles in the covered Ikea parking lot, we were afraid that you wouldn't know which car to follow."

"And yet they spotted you," Kramer said. "And your lives were endangered, further distracting us from our mission."

Budge picked up their defense. "But we subdued our abductors, told you where to find them. Then we escaped, helping the operation!"

Iris regarded him with a raised eyebrow. *We?*

"And came into direct contact with the man I forbade you to approach," Kramer said.

Jim Dugan folded his arms across his enormous chest and spoke up for the first time. "Don't you mean the patsy? You knew before my plane touched down this morning that my son was safe. I only agreed to this goddam suicide mission to save Jimmy. What you did was unethical. My lawyer will have a field day with this."

Kramer held up a hand to placate him. "Maybe it was a gray area, a judgment call. We needed to catch Westbrook in the act to make your accusations stick."

"And maybe what *we* did was also a gray area," Iris argued. "I gave you a lot of information to help you get this far. I'm sorry if we slowed down the investigation today, but we were trying to help."

Kramer held up his hands. "I don't have time to deal with the two of you. Into the van. Dugan, you'll go with Agent Monroe in the Kia. We've located Westbrook and need to make an arrest now."

79

Trent disconnected the call from Jimbo and ran out the front door of the abandoned nursing home. He was desperate to find Edward and tell him about this new threat. Jimbo's lawyer would expose Trent's deeds if his old friend didn't emerge alive from this meeting. Edward couldn't eliminate Jimbo until his fixer came up with a work-around.

As Trent approached the woods next to the parking lot, he waved his arms and called out loudly, "It's just me. I need to speak with you."

A few seconds later, Trent heard a rustling above him and watched his chief of security climb down from a tree, a black AR-15 rifle slung over his shoulder. "You shouldn't be out here. Dugan will arrive at any moment."

It surprised Trent to see sweat marks under Edward's armpits—an unprecedented lack of cool that made him uneasy. He relayed his new information about Dugan's threat and watched as Edward's expression turned to stone.

"This isn't good. So, how is Dugan supposed to contact the lawyer to confirm that he's alive?" Edward asked.

"By phone, I guess. But even if we can grab Jimbo and force him to make that call, the lawyer will find out soon enough, once good old Jimbo disappears. He'd release the affidavit then."

Edward put his fingertips to his forehead and frowned. "We need to abort. There's no time to come up with a counterplan. And I've been trying to reach Jorge and Smitty. They picked up the reporter and that damn architect but aren't answering their phones. The GPS on their car shows them stopped at the back side of Riverbend Country Club. We need to get out of here fast."

Trent felt his heart pounding hard against his ribs, a rush of fear. This couldn't be happening! Not to him. Edward would surely figure something out.

He and Edward had driven together in a small nondescript car they'd left hidden deep in the woods. As they started walking along a path in that direction, they heard the whoop-whooping of helicopter blades above them. Then the command over a loudspeaker, surprisingly sharp and loud. "This is the FBI. Trent Westbrook and Edward Weber, you are under arrest. Come out in the open with your hands up."

Trent watched over his shoulder as a white van streaked into the parking lot. Agents with drawn rifles emerged and ran toward him. He looked around for guidance from Edward, but his chief of security was nowhere to be found.

80

While the action unfolded outside the former nursing home in Canton, Iris and Budge huddled in the white van with the two tech agents, monitoring an array of display screens. They watched Trent Westbrook being led away in handcuffs to another FBI car. Four of his accomplices had been captured earlier, but Iris and Budge overheard the techs saying that Westbrook's right-hand security man, Edward Weber, was in the wind. A BOLO had been issued for him.

A few hours later, when the van arrived back at FBI headquarters in Chelsea, Iris and Budge followed agents into separate interrogation rooms. Iris was offered a dry ham-and-cheese sandwich and a Styrofoam cup of truly terrible coffee while she waited. For two plus hours, she had no phone or anything else to distract her, only her worries. Was Kramer going to arrest her? Would she be allowed to call Sterling, her attorney brother, to bail her out? Finally, Agent Kramer and a young woman introduced as Agent Monroe entered the room. Iris recognized her as the one who hid in the back of Dugan's first car. Bummer of a day for her.

Kramer instructed Iris to go over every tiny thing that had

happened in the last seven hours. She left off the part about eavesdropping on the agents' meeting at the airport and emphasized her personal stake in finding the person who had kidnapped her the previous day. She skidded lightly over her revelation to Dugan about his son being safe. After an hour of questioning and the signing of a statement about her actions, Iris was relieved when Kramer let her off with a stern warning. Evidently some of her phone messages had been useful, so he decided not to refer her to the federal prosecutor for obstruction of justice.

It was 4 p.m. by the time Iris was escorted back out to the lobby and given her phone and purse. She called an Uber, then noticed Budge still there, sitting on one of the plastic visitors' chairs.

He looked up from his phone. "So, Reid. Did you get the bamboo-under-the-fingernails treatment too?" The lobby receptionist looked up and glared at him from behind her plexiglass barrier.

"No, Agent Kramer thanked me for my bravery in taking down two of Westbrook's confederates. Why? Did he give you a hard time?"

"About that." Budge looked suddenly sheepish. "I'd like to thank you for punching the bad guy in the nuts today."

"You mean for saving your life?"

"Yeah. I never thought things would get that gnarly. You've got some impressive chops."

"You're welcome, Budge." Iris felt exhausted and wanted to get home.

"I've submitted my story about Westbrook and Dugan to my editor. Kramer made me delete any mention of our contributions to the drama. But the confirmation about Dugan's part in the two murders in your building should vindicate you from the podcast fallout."

"That's a relief. Okay—my Uber is here. See you around, Budge."

When She got home, Sheba waddled out to meet her, wagging her tail. Luc was downstairs cooking for a full house, so Iris went to the kitchen and found some scraps of chicken to toss in Sheba's bowl. After pouring herself a balloon glass of St. Émilion, she brought it into the living room and settled on the sofa. It was too early to check the local TV news, so she opened her laptop on the coffee table, and went to the *BostonGlobe.com* website to see if Budge's account of the take-down had been posted.

It was the breaking story: **Congressman Trent Westbrook and Fugitive James Dugan Implicated in Deaths of Homeless Teen and Carpenter Attacked in Harvard Square Museum.** Iris skimmed through the article which made it sound as if Special Agent Gene Kramer of the FBI had teamed up with Lieutenant Joseph Garcia of the Cambridge Police Department to put together the pieces of the cold case and the recent assault. The story was sketchy on details at this early point, but the FBI's dramatic capture of Westbrook in Canton was featured prominently. Budge also managed to work in Westbrook's ownership of several properties purchased through shell companies. Enough to give the voters pause. She felt equally relieved and resentful that there was no mention of her role in figuring out what had happened.

Iris clicked over to the website for the Tamarindo Surf Camp in Costa Rica. The all-inclusive two-week program promised to turn beginners into competent surfers by the end of fourteen days. Not all the people in the glossy pictures looked young and nubile. The instructors spoke English, and the accommodations and meals were described as luxurious. In short, it looked good. And, most important, Luc wanted to do this. With her.

He wouldn't be finished with tonight's dinner service for another six hours, but Iris was longing to see him. She'd give him the edited version of today's adventure, the one that didn't include guns being pointed at her. Iris went into the bedroom and set her phone alarm to wake her so the two of them could talk when he came upstairs. She lay down on the bed in her clothes and was asleep before she could count half-a-dozen sheep.

Iris tapped off the alarm at 11 p.m., got up, and made herself a cup of coffee. She turned the lights in the living room and hallway on low and reread the surf camp article in the magazine Luc had showed her a few days before. The more she thought about it, the more she was warming to the idea of the trip.

It was midnight before she heard Luc's footsteps on the stairs. Iris met him on the landing.

"I didn't think you'd still be up," he said when he saw her. "How did everything go on your stakeout? Did you restrain yourself from murdering Budge?"

"Barely." She led him to the living room where they sank onto the sofa. Iris filled him in on the FBI agents bringing in Trent Westbrook and Jim Dugan for the murders in the museum.

"And you're still in one piece. You stayed out of danger. See—you can do it." Luc leaned over and kissed her. He glanced down at the coffee table. "Have you been reading the magazine article?"

"Yeah. The camp looks great, it really does. Let's go for the full two weeks. I'm sorry I seemed so hesitant."

Luc's expression turned serious as he reached for her hand. "We can't let our work take over our lives. I told you why my marriage to Gia failed, right?"

"You said you were always preoccupied with the restaurant in Rome and too much distance grew between you."

"It would break me if that happened with us, Iris. I want more to my world than just the restaurant. I want to spend time with you. To go on adventures together. To have a good life."

She stood, pulled him to his feet, and wrapped her arms around him. With her cheek against his chest, she could feel his heartbeat. "I want that too. Let's go to bed."

81

Over the next two weeks, Iris eagerly followed the news about the fates of Dugan and Westbrook. Sterling was happy to lawyer-splain any terms or technicalities she didn't fully understand.

Jim Dugan's shark of an attorney reinforced his reputation. In exchange for his client's testimony against Trent Westbrook, Dugan would spend a mere two years in prison for the involuntary manslaughter of Carl Nowak, so he'd be out while Jimmy was still young. Dugan had been seventeen when he'd been an accessory to Sam Parker's murder years before, so his juvenile sentence was rolled into those two years.

The charges for Trent Westbrook were still being tallied. Since he'd been eighteen years old when he instigated the murder of Sam Parker, bringing along a stun gun which demonstrated premeditation, Westbrook would be tried as an adult for that crime and would spend most, if not all, of the rest of his life behind bars. His role in Carl Nowak's death and the series of kidnappings of Jimmy, Iris and Budge was still being defined.

Edward Weber had been caught trying to leave the country in a small plane and had promptly turned on his old boss in exchange for a lighter sentence. He was able to fill in the various gaps about the kidnappings and knew details about Westbrook's lucrative scheme to use federal funds to purchase and build homeless shelters on properties he owned anonymously. However, Weber remained silent about Kegs Linkletter's death, since he had played such an outsized part in it.

While Iris felt some satisfaction in seeing Sam and Carl's killers put behind bars, there was one more thing she still needed to attend to.

Iris set off from home on a brisk November morning to pick up a parcel from the newly opened jewelry store she had designed. She carried the small but heavy package through Harvard Square to the museum.

They were all assembled inside, near the old staircase: Sam's friend Judith from the soup kitchen, Milo and his crew, and Gail Nowak. A section of the subfloor had been lifted to expose the joists where Sam Parker's remains had been found.

Iris handed the box to Milo, and he unwrapped it. He stared sadly at the object, then read out loud the etched words on the top bronze plaque: Carl Nowak, Rest in Peace, brother, 1991-2023. There was a small picture of a motorcycle at the bottom. He handed it to Carl's wife. Gail ran her finger over the words and pursed her lips tightly to keep from crying.

Milo held up the second plaque so everyone could see it: Sam Parker, Taken from this World too soon, 1984-2003. A guitar was drawn at the bottom of his plaque. Milo handed this one to Judith whose cheeks were already streaked with tears.

Dewey and the rest of the crew stood in a half-circle, hands folded in front of them, eyes cast downward at the makeshift memorial. Milo got down on his hands and knees and pulled a small tack hammer from his tool belt. He reached up to Gail for the first plaque. She sighed as she passed it down. Using matching bronze nails, he carefully secured the marker to the side of a joist through the tiny holes that had been drilled in each corner.

Judith let out a muffled sob as she handed Milo the second plaque. He nailed it next to Carl's, then stood up and said a few words. "No one but us will know that these mementos are here below the marble floor. But we'll remember these two good men whose lives were cut short unfairly. Their murderers have now been found and they will pay for their crimes. But we will miss our friends. Whenever we want to feel close to their spirits, we'll have this private spot to visit."

Iris felt goosebumps. It was probably the emotion of the occasion, but she could swear she felt two ghostly presences in the room with them.

AN INDEPENDENT AUTHOR'S REQUEST

I hope you enjoyed Iris's latest adventure. Please help support an independent writer by leaving a review on the site where you purchased this book. Your comments and reviews are valuable, and I would love to hear your feedback.

Thank you, and I hope you're looking forward to the next installment in the Iris Reid Mystery Series.

Please "like" my Fan Page on Facebook and say hello:

https://www.facebook.com/authorsusancory

For early notification of further Iris Reid Mystery Series books, please sign up on my webpage: www.susancory.com

Thanks again!

Susan Cory

ACKNOWLEDGMENTS

I would like to thank the following people for their invaluable feedback. My heartfelt gratitude goes to Denise Dilanni, a Senior Executive Producer, for her insights into film crews and some of their mechanics. Any mistakes or characterizations are purely mine.

As always, I'd like to thank my writing group: Millicent Eidson, M.R. Dimond, and Amy Reade for their guidance and support. I am indebted to my eagle-eyed beta readers: Janice Schupak, Ellen Kolten and John Baird Rogers.

And last, but not least, I'm grateful to Dan Tenney for his critical editing.

To all the readers who have told me they've enjoyed my stories: I love hearing from you on Facebook and in your reviews. Your messages encourage me to keep writing.

Made in the USA
Middletown, DE
30 September 2024